DAISY

BOOK FIVE

In Our Mother's Garden

By

Joyce Humphrey Cares

Mainstream Romance

DEDICATION

To

My son Mark

BACK COVER

At a young age, Daisy O'Malley discovered she was clairvoyant. Her ability to communicate with the dead and travel back in time hadn't surfaced for many years. However, events are about to change.

Resting in a community gazebo, she re-evaluates her life in Hollywood, California. Deep in thought she is surprised when a mist suddenly envelopes her and she is whisked back into the roaring twenties, and the ghosts become real again.

Her journey into 1922 lures her to an upscale Hollywood neighborhood, where she seeks to find out if there is trouble behind an open door of one of the cottages. Entering the bungalow, she discovers a man lying dead in a pool of blood.

With the past ripped opened, she becomes a witness to life during the Eighteenth Amendment. She is drawn into an era of prosperity filled with bootleg alcohol, wild parties, jazz, speakeasies, and the increase of crime that came with the rise of the Mafia in the United States.

When Detective Jack Donovan arrives on the scene, Daisy works with him to find a killer. Pulled into a dangerous liaison, she becomes entangled in an inescapable web of lies, secrets, and cold-blooded murder. Together, they dig into the dark secrets of the dead man's life and the women who loved him.

DAISY

*"...Two souls are sometimes created together
before they are born."*
F. Scott Fitzgerald

CHAPTER ONE

Los Angeles, California
January 2018

Mammoth, white block letters, standing on stilts in the rolling hills of Griffith State Park, spelled out Hollywood. The sign was the first landmark Daisy O'Malley saw as her plane approached Los Angeles Airport. Relaxed in jeans and boots, she sat in the last seat of first class. A warm glow flowed through her. Employed in a glamorous profession in the district bound by the Sunset Strip to the west and the Hollywood Bowl, and the famous sign to the east, known as the movie industry, made her smile. The dream of making it big in Tinsel Town was about to come true. Accepting extra work, then small walk-on parts, finally paid off. She landed a significant role in a western.

But do I really want a career in Hollywood? This thought had been running through her mind as the plane soared from Maine to California. She had second thoughts. After her Christmas visit and the wonderful time she had with her daughter, Emily, and her family, she was not sure it had been worth leaving Maine a few years ago for her lengthy rise in the film business.

She missed the snow-covered ground of winter, the sound of the rolling waves of the Atlantic Ocean hitting the cliff at high tide in front of the gray Victorian home and sitting in front of a roaring fire. She loved listening to the cracking of pinecones and seeing their colored sparks when thrown into the fire. She was sure if she stayed, instead of escaping to the land of fantasy, Emily's father, never her husband, could have worked out any arrangements where both of them would have time with their daughter.

She hoped her house near Hollywood would be empty when she returned. She divorced her cheating husband and told him to move out while she was gone. The marriage was one of the biggest blunders she'd ever made. When she arrived in Hollywood years ago, she became caught up in the glamor of the film world and married after knowing him only two weeks. He was charming and devilishly handsome. It didn't take long for her to find out he was a womanizer and a ne'er-do-well.

All in all, the trip back home gave her a new slant on life. She did a lot of soul searching while walking on the sandy beach. Hearing the wave's crash against the rocky coast mesmerized her. She stayed in the family home with Emily, who lived with Daisy's twin sister, Violet, and Violet's husband. She and her daughter spent every minute together. She made peace with her sister, and their problems of the past forgotten. The trip was a huge success.

Maybe I'll go home for good. I'm ready even if I've finally obtained a large part in a film. A war of emotion raged within.

The beep of the seatbelt sign startled her. She buckled up and pressed her foot into the floor when the rush of the plane filled the air. She smiled. *There's no brake under my foot.* Grabbing the armrest, she held on tightly when the plane hit the tarmac and bounced.

After the plane rolled and stopped at the jet-way, she gathered up her jacket and purse. She threw the jacket over her shoulders, opened her purse, and searched for her sunglasses. *Here they are.* She slipped them on and pushed them up on the bridge of her nose. Opening the overhead bin, she pulled out her hat, shoved it on her head, and smiled at the crew as she deplaned.

On the walk to baggage claim, she signed autographs for the few people who recognized her, even though she tried to hide behind dark glasses and a floppy hat pulled low on her forehead to conceal her auburn hair. She smiled at the teenage girl who approached her.

"Please, Miss O'Malley, will you sign my notebook? I see you in all the movie magazines."

Daisy looked at her. *She reminds me of my daughter, Emily.* "Of course. What's your name?"

"Suzie."

I hope she doesn't believe all the stories she reads in those magazines. A thoughtful smile curved Daisy's mouth as she wrote quickly. She watched the girl's face light up as she read out loud the note.

"Never give up, Suzie, and you'll get your dream. If you want it."

Suzie hugged the notebook to her chest. "I won't, Miss O'Malley. I won't. I promise."

Daisy waved and hurried to the down escalator. Passing the baggage claim area, she rushed to the Departures door. She weaved through the sea of people scurrying about like a blanket of ants, either retrieving luggage or leaving the terminal to catch a ride to their next destination. When she heard her name called, she sighed relief. Looking up, she saw her driver approaching.

"Good morning, John," she called and waved.

Reaching her, he took her elbow and guided her past the crowd and through the sliding glass doors. He ushered her toward the waiting limo at the curbside.

She stood back. After John opened the back door, she slid into the back seat. "Please leave the door open," she said, pushing her baggage tickets into his hand. "The cases are hot pink, and there are two of them."

"Hey, Buddy." The airport policeman blew his whistle, walking toward her driver. "You can't park here," he yelled.

Daisy watched John pay no attention to the policeman as he rushed past him through the glass doors and walked to the carousel and the three-deep crowd in front of it. Luckily, space opened, and he edged his way to the front of the line of people. She saw him keep his eye on the luggage tumble and bump as they rolled on the conveyer belt.

She saw him glanced at the claim tickets when two hot pink suitcases came through the rubber strips toward him. *He's got them.* She thought when he dragged them off the moving belt and carefully matched the tickets to the tickets in his hand. She smiled as he pulled up the handles, and hurried back to the limo.

Twisting the small, gold ball in her right ear, Daisy leaned out of the limo door and called to the airport guard. "Sorry. He'll only be a minute." She pointed to the carousel. "See, he has my luggage already and is on his way back. We'll be gone in a second."

The policeman bent and glanced at her. "Oh, it's you, Miss O'Malley." His eyebrows rose. He pushed his cap to the back of his head and smiled. His grin showed a line of slightly yellowed, crooked teeth. "My daughter loves the autographed photo you sent to her. Thanks again."

Daisy smiled. She noticed his suit was wrinkled, and one leg smudged with dirt. *Must be a tough job.*

He leaned closer to her and whispered, "The bosses check every once in a while. So, I have to enforce the rules." He sighed. "Sorry. Make sure you're gone by the time I get back." He strolled on the sidewalk to the end of the Delta Airlines section, blew his whistle and motioned with a wave for illegally parked cars to move on.

"See. He's here now," she called to his back. She pulled off her hat and laid it on the seat beside her.

Hearing the pop of the trunk, Daisy leaned back and closed the door. She smiled as passengers and drivers craned their necks, trying to see who sat behind the tinted windows of the limo. She waited for John to turn the key in the ignition, step on the accelerator, and slip into the flow of traffic, leaving the airport, before she knocked on the dark, glass partition. "John."

He pushed a button on the top of the console next to his seat. "Yes, Miss."

She started to cough as the screen slid down.

"Are you all right, Miss?" He looked over his shoulder.

The driver of a car in the lane alongside the limo honked several times. John quickly turned the wheel and moved back to where he belonged.

"Yes, but I developed a cold in Maine. I have a cough I can't seem to get rid of." She raised a hand and cleared her throat. "Please stop at the mall near my condo. I need to pick up a prescription my doctor called in and a few other things at the drug store." She sighed.

"No problem, Miss."

"Did my husband, Andre, move out? I told him to be gone when I got home."

"Yes, Miss, he's gone."

"Thank goodness. Emily never liked her stepfather. It will be much nicer when she comes to visit." Daisy didn't share with John her new thought of leaving Hollywood and going home to Maine.

She looked out the window as the driver inched through the city's morning rush hour traffic. It wasn't long before she watched him turn off the highway onto a side street. He drove through a residential area toward the mall. Dried out Christmas trees lay on the curbs in front of homes, waiting for the trash collectors. A faint breeze picked up their dry, brown needles, scattering them on the sidewalks and in between the blades of grass of the lawns.

John guided the limo up Westlake Drive and turned into the northeast side of the mall's parking lot. Daisy pushed the button to open her window. "It's a beautiful January day, but cool." She smiled.

Sun shone through billowing white clouds. Pathways lined with palm trees and gardens of purple lilacs, red Amaryllis, azaleas, Bird of Paradise, and bromeliads filled the upscale shopping area. The fronds of the palm trees swayed in the breeze. Outdoor cafes with heaters worked at full force, blasting heat to take the chill from the air. Patrons were scattered at the tables and chairs of the restaurants mixed among shops and boutiques.

Avoiding shoppers wandering across the streets, without looking at the traffic, John pulled toward the curb at the top of a hill. He slowed when he reached the shop with an Apothecary sign hanging over the door.

Daisy raised the window and waited for the limo to roll to a complete stop, and the ignition key clicked off. "Please don't get out, John. I won't be long. Wait for me behind the gazebo across the street." She stared at the dark clouds moving quickly over the sun. "It looks as if we're going to have a downpour." *Hopefully not before I finish my shopping and get back to the limo.* She glanced at the seat. Opening her purse for her credit card, she stuffed the card into her pocket. *I better take my purse, just in case.* Grabbing it, she slung it over her shoulder.

She pushed open the car door just as the sky opened. Jumping from the limo, she reached back, slammed the door, and ran. She pulled open the door of the drug store, shook off the drops of water collected on her head and clothing, and walked to the back of the store. A sign, reading Pharmacy, hung in front of an opened window. On the way, she picked up a jar of multivitamins and some cough medicine. *I should have taken these vitamins before now. I would be in better health and not so fatigued from lack of sleep and skipping meals. I didn't catch up with my rest on vacation. Who cares? Spending time with Emily and joining her when she ate junk food was okay. Sleeping in the twin beds and talking into the wee hours of the morning was just like when I was young and had sleepovers with my friends. It was so good to see her.* She smiled.

Daisy walked to the sign, Pick Up Here. "I have a prescription waiting, O'Malley," she said to the man in a white coat.

"First name?" the pharmacist asked.

"Daisy."

"Address and date of birth?"

She rattled off the requested information, slipped her credit card into the chip slot, and waited. After signing the slip the druggist pushed toward her, she stuffed the card in her pocket. He put her purchases in a white paper bag. Handing it to her, he smiled.

"Thanks." Daisy grabbed the bag and started to the front of the shop.

"The prescription is for ten days. Take all ten days of the antibiotic, or you'll be right back here," the pharmacist called to her as she ran toward the front door.

January 2, 1922
Hollywood, California

A soft gasp escaped her when she peered into the glass of the front door. Heavy fog swirled and shifted, hiding the street in front of her and the gazebo. Squinting, she pushed her nose against the glass door and searched for her limo. She stood for a moment searching for John and the limo, but it was nowhere in sight. *The rain has stopped, but the fog hasn't disappeared. I'll wait a few minutes and see if it clears.*

Hearing someone clear their throat, she turned her head. "Sorry." She smiled and stepped to the side so the man behind her could pass. *My goodness, he doesn't fit in with his dark suit, starched white shirt, tie, and hat. He's not dressed like most Californians in casual shorts or trousers, Tommy Bahama shirts, and flip-flops.*

She watched him throw some coins on the counter, reach in front of her, and grab a newspaper from the news rack. He pushed open the door and hurried into the lifting fog. She thought she could see a faint outline of homes behind the gazebo.

Daisy glanced at the copy of the morning edition of the Los Angeles Times in the news rack. She stared at the date. "It can't be happening. Not now. Why am I being called back to January 2, 1922," she whispered.

She looked out at the weather. The mist had disappeared. Pushing through the door, she walked into the street and looked in the direction of the gazebo. The bright sun beat down on her. The droplets of water, still floating in the air, vanished quickly. She ran her hand through her hair. Capturing escaping damp tendrils sticking to her cheek, she pressed them behind her ear. She dug her hand in her pocket and reached for a hairband, stopped walking, and pulled her long hair back into a ponytail.

Daisy stared. Her limo was not standing behind the gazebo. It was gone. A cast-iron fence and gate surrounded the gazebo in front of her. *Poor John, he must wonder where I am. He has no idea I've slipped into 1922.* She stood on a black-top street and wrapped her arms around herself. A breeze picked up, drying her tendrils. Daisy glanced over her shoulder. A field of emerald grass and wildflowers filled the space where the parking lot and stores had been. She bent and looked closely at the flowers. She wished she knew their names. She sighed. Gardening had never been something she enjoyed. *Maybe when I get back to Maine.*

Through the bars in front of her, she saw a heavyset man in overhauls, a T-shirt, work shoes, and a large, straw hat shading his face. He knelt at the flower gardens, surrounding a gazebo, pulling weeds. He tossed the unwanted plants on the tarp beside him. Looking up, he stopped weeding and watched her. He smiled when he heard the gate squeak and scrape as Daisy pushed on it and slid it open.

Walking through the gate, she let it creep back on its own and close with a loud clang. She noticed the gardener didn't seem to mind the broken tranquility or interruption in his work. He smiled and waved. The sun bounced off a front gold tooth.

She waved back and looked up. A sign hung from the roof of the gazebo. The name of the exclusive area, South Alvarado Court, was printed in large black letters. In smaller letters was written, "The favorite residential neighborhood for motion picture people." Wisteria hung over the roof of the gazebo, like an umbrella. Two bees chased each other around the purple flowers. Beyond the gardens and gazebo stood eight two-unit homes.

The up-scale, two-story bungalows with white stucco walls and orange tile roofs gave the homes a Spanish look. They were built in a U-shape around the backside of the gazebos. The houses, tucked behind dark, green hedges, were set back from a gravel road on one lane. The cement front paths of each home sat on pristine front lawns, and led from two stone gate posts, with the gates long gone, to front oak doors.

Daisy stared at the cottages with black numbers nailed on the front of each entrance. The door of cottage 4B stood ajar, exposing a dark interior. Daisy walked up the sidewalk, noticing the brass nameplate over the doorbell. It read Desmond Cunningham Walsh. Beneath the lowest hinge of the door sat a milk bottle. Moisture dripped down the glass, leaving a small puddle of water on the porch, as the milk warmed.

She pushed on the bell and called, "Mr. Walsh, are you home?" She waited. After the chimes stopped, she eased open the door a little. When no one answered the bell or her voice, she pushed the door all the way open, stepped inside a few feet, and glanced around. Seeing no one, she called again. "Hello. Is anybody home?"

With her hand, she pressed harder on the door and pushed when it swung back toward her. It bumped against the wall with a thump. *That should get someone's attention.* Seeing nothing but a dark interior, she stepped further into the hallway onto a black and gray, marble floor. Still calling out the name on the brass plate, she jumped when the door closed behind her. There was no answer. She stood in the pitch-black.

Staring into the darkness, she ran her hand over a stucco wall beside her, hunting for a light switch. Finally finding one, she flicked on a light. The illumination was so dim that she looked up to make sure she had switched on the hall light. A round chandelier with candle-shaped bulbs hung from the ceiling. Several of the bulbs were not lit. Ahead and to her left, she saw a staircase covered with an Oriental rug. Books were piled haphazardly on a bench next to the stairs. A grandfather clock stood against the wall beyond the staircase and next to open double doors, its pendulum swinging quietly. She leaned forward. A baby grand piano occupied most of the room with the pair of dark doors. A door beneath the stairs was closed. *That must lead to the kitchen.*

Tiptoeing over the marble floor, she peeked into the open doorway of the first room on her right. Long, dark drapes covered all the windows, except the glass French doors across from the entrance of the room. The partially opened doors led to a patio showing the signs of cool weather. Dried leaves covered patio chairs and a table. The sheer drapes covering the French doors blew in a breeze. A tree's leaves and branches hung over the patio and outside the doors. They helped shade most of the sun trying to peek into the room. In the breeze, they tapped gently on the glass doors. Though the light was dim, she was still able to walk into the room and explore her surroundings.

A mahogany desk and chair occupied the wall to her right. The desk chair was pulled back, and one back leg was pushed into the wall. It looked as if someone had left it in a hurry. Over the chair was a photo of President Warren G. Harding with a tall man holding a golf club. *The man must be the owner of this house.* She took a few steps to the desk and looked at the papers on top. An opened checkbook and a fountain pen laid on top. Next to the checkbook was a half-completed tax return. She leaned over and glanced at the papers. Under salary, 38,000 dollars was listed. *A trivial amount now, but in 1922 a substantial salary.*

Autographed and framed photographs, mostly of women, lined the wall. On her left, a large couch sat in front of a fireplace and behind a low coffee table. Wingback chairs flanked either end of the table. Two empty martini glasses perched on the coffee table. The ruby glow of the embers on the hearth flickered through the glasses. Two toothpicks sat next to the glasses. One still poked into an olive.

A Tiffany lamp and a candlestick rotary dial phone sat on the table with a straight chair near the end of the couch. The receiver of the phone hung by its cord in front of the table. It swung back and forth. The buzz of the dial tone from the hanging receiver echoed through the room.

A gramophone occupied a table near the doors to the patio. The scraping noise of a needle moving back and forth on a vinyl record on the turntable added to the sound of the phone. The room had an eerie feeling. Daisy looked up. She studied photos hanging on either side of the fireplace. The buzzing and scratching of the gramophone began to bother her, but she knew better than to touch anything.

"Something is wrong," she whispered. Glancing closer at the coffee table in front of the couch, she noticed the distorted stub of a burned-out candle. It had melted like a pancake in a glass dish sitting in the middle of the coffee table.

Then she saw it and screamed. "Oh, no." The silhouette of a figure laid on the floor. The still body was wedged between the couch and coffee table.

"Oh, no," she yelled again. She leaned over the back of the couch and stared closer at the body lying face down on the floor. She moved slowly around the couch and bent down. *It's a man.* Threading her hand to the front of his neck, she pressed on the carotid artery. *No pulse.* In the dim light, she saw blood pooled on the Oriental rug, around his chest. *I need to call the police. I'm sure there's no 911 in 1922. What's their number? I guess the operator can help me.*

Startled, she stood but didn't move an inch. The pounding of feet on the stairs, coming from the second floor, shocked her. *I have to find somewhere to hide.* Looking around the room, she stared at the desk. The footsteps were in the hallway, then in the room. They stopped. A dark shadow loomed on the wall in front of her. There was no longer time to run and dive behind the desk. She panicked and froze.

A hand, with an iron grip, grabbed her arm and pushed, shoving her out of the way. An icy fear twisted around her heart as she was thrown against the wall. Her head slammed into a group of the hanging photographs. The shadow attached to the hand continued running through the room toward the French doors. Daisy heard the crash of a something knocked over as the person left by the open terrace doors. She was alone. The person was gone. A pain shot through her head after hitting the wall. The room whirled, causing dizziness. Her legs buckled and she lost balance. She slid to the floor. Glass shattered around her feet. A cool breeze covered her before losing consciousness.

CHAPTER TWO

Daisy blinked, trying to focus her gaze. Deep lines appeared between her eyes. She inhaled and exhaled deeply until she felt strong enough to raise her head and shoulders while leaning on her elbows. She stared at the ceiling, still trying to focus. Her eyes darted back and forth nervously. *Where am I? How long have I been unconscious? Not very long, I'm sure.*

The sound at the front door startled Daisy. A key turned in the lock, making her heart quicken. The hinges squeaked when the door pushed open. Footsteps of leathered-sole shoes tapped briskly on the tile floor of the hallway. Through hazy vision, she saw a man standing in the doorway of the room where she lay.

He threw up his hands when he saw her. The milk bottle he held slipped from his fingers and crashed to the floor. Pieces of glass spewed over the floor and scattered in the pool of milk around his feet. His piercing shriek sent a chill through her.

She blinked her eyes again and waited. Finally, she felt alert enough to raise herself. She pushed herself into a sitting position and tried to orient herself. The band holding her hair back broke, letting her long auburn hair hang gracefully over her shoulders and face, clouding some of her vision that wasn't already blurred by hitting her head. She stared at the figure in front of her. At last, her vision began focusing correctly. She tucked stray hair strands behind her ears. "Where am I?" Straightening her shoulders, she cleared her throat. A wave of dizziness overcame her. She fell back and landed against the couch. Careful not to move so she wouldn't land in the glass around her, she sat very still.

"I'm Mr. Walsh's valet, servant, Henry Peavey. "Who are you? Why are you here?" he shrieked. His eyes bulged from their sockets.

"I'm Daisy O'Malley. I'm an actress." She hung onto the couch and pushed herself to a standing position. Still feeling dizzy, she held onto the back of the sofa. "I was walking by and saw the door open. I thought something might be wrong, so I let myself in and looked around to make sure everything was all right." She waited. When she was strong enough to stand on her own, she moved away from the couch, avoiding the milk and glass. She started walking toward the valet but stopped when the milk rolled toward her.

"I come here every morning, at this time, to prepare breakfast before I start my day working on anything Mr. Walsh needs." He walked towards Daisy. His feet crunched in the pieces of splintered glass. "Are you here to talk with Mr. Walsh about his new movie?"

"Something like that." She decided it would be too confusing to tell him the whole story. He wouldn't believe her anyhow. She would probably be inviting a one-way ticket to the funny farm if he repeated her story to the authorities. She moved, trying to block his view of the floor in front of the couch. She couldn't stand to hear him shriek again. She twisted the gold ball in her right ear. Her vision now wholly cleared, she studied the man who wore a brown, herringbone newsboy hat, tweed vest over a white shirt, and nickers. His skin was dark.

"Are you hiding something?" He came closer to her, leaned forward, and stretched his body. Looking around her, he stared.

"Don't scream." She moved to lift her hands, ready to cover her ears, if he screeched again.

"What's hap…pen…to Mr. Walsh?" he asked. His hands shook as he backed toward the entrance of the room, away from Daisy. Shoving his hands in his pockets, he hunched his shoulders forward and moved back slowly to Daisy so he could again peer at the body on the floor.

"If this is Mr. Walsh, I think he's dead. There's blood on the floor around his chest, and I couldn't feel a pulse." Not quite recovered, she moved slowly, letting him look at the body. She reached for the back of the couch, next to her, to steady herself as she stood. Glancing at the legs of her jeans, she saw blood. *I must have stained them when I bent down to feel for the pulse.*

His eyes opened so wide they looked like they might pop out of his head. Crunching on the glass, he ran to the front door. "Mr. Walsh is dead. Mr. Walsh is dead," he screamed.

"Ah," Daisy paused. Digging into her pocket, she pulled a handkerchief from her jeans. She rubbed at the stain. *Bloodstains on my clothes will probably make me a suspect.*

"What's that noise?" she asked. The blaring noise of sirens got louder as they approached the house. She watched Peavey's lips move. The sirens drowned out his voice.

The earsplitting squeal of brakes as the autos screeched to a stop replaced the sirens piercing the air.

"What did you say?" she asked again.

"One of the neighbors must have called the police when they heard me scream."

Daisy ambled to the front door. She stood staring as the two men in plainclothes rushed to the house. She moved so they could enter the bungalow's hallway. Several uniformed policemen followed while others stood at the front door and on the steps of the house. Daisy was surprised when she saw the press with paper and pencils, and cameras rush up the sidewalk pavers. Held back by the police, they retreated and camped out on the front lawn. She slowly followed the plainclothes men to the room where the body lay. She stood in the doorway.

"What am I walking over?" the older policeman asked when he heard the crunching sound of glass under his feet upon entering the room.

"Glass," Daisy said.

"I'm Enzo Sullivan." He smiled. "Italian mother and Irish father who dropped the O when he landed at Ellis Island in New York City."

"Detective Lieutenant Sullivan, and this is Detective Jack Donovan." He continued. "What's going on here? We got a call someone was screaming about someone being dead."

"It's my employer, Mr. Walsh. He's dead," Mr. Peavey screamed. Drops of water slid down his cheeks. "I dropped the milk bottle and smashed lots of pieces. I'll clean it up." He turned and started to walk to the door behind the stairs.

"Leave it until we're finished with our questions and examination of the scene," Sullivan said gruffly.

"And who are you? What are you doing here?" He stared at Daisy.

She looked into the dark, brown eyes of a tall, overweight man. A fedora hat perched on the back of his head accentuated his round face. The rest of his attire, a tie with the knot loosened, three-piece suit, a white shirt, and an overcoat, were wrinkled. His stomach hung over his belt.

Avoiding the milk, she walked closer to the police and the body. "I'm Daisy O'Malley. I was walking by and saw the door open. I let myself in, thinking something might be wrong. I was right. A man was lying on the floor. The man right there." She pointed to the body. "I was bent over to see if he was dead or alive. I stood up so I could walk to the front door and call a neighbor, but I didn't get that far. Someone ran by me and knocked me down. My head hit the wall, and I lost consciousness. I don't know how long I was out. I suspect it was only for a few minutes. I was just coming around when Mr. Peavey arrived."

"Do you know where the person came from who knocked you down?"

"I think whoever it was came from the second floor. I heard footsteps pounding on the stairs. I'm sure the person was as surprised to see me as I was to see them when they ran into this room. When my head met the wall after pushed, everything went black."

"Do you know where the person went? Male or female?"

"No, Lieutenant Sullivan. I don't know if the person was male or female. But, they must have left by the glass doors to the patio, because I heard a crash. Something got knocked over before I passed out." She pointed to the overturned straight chair in front of the doors leading to the terrace. "Now, I can see it must have been that straight chair." She pointed to the chair next to the table with the Tiffany lamp. "It wasn't turned over when I first came into the room. Thank goodness the lamp didn't fall. It's a beautiful antique and probably was quite expensive."

She glanced at the younger man standing next to the lieutenant. His powerful, well-muscled body fit perfectly into his tan trousers with navy suspenders, a vest, and , rumpled white shirt. He ran his hand through his black hair, still wet from a morning shower, messing up already tousled hair. His eyes were the dark blue of the sea. They were alert and penetrating. He did not attempt to hide the fact he watched her. Walking to the French doors, he looked around. She noticed his eyes crinkled as a smile began at the corners of his mouth. A dazzling display of white teeth showed when his lips parted.

Daisy took a long look. "You got here quickly." She smiled at him. Ruggedly handsome, his looks made her senses spin and heart beat a little faster. The smell of his aftershave tantalized her.

"The station is close by." Pushing his sunglasses to the top of his head, he peered at her intently. "Miss O'Malley, do you need to sit?" Reaching for the chair at the French doors, Detective Donovan righted it. "Your skin is as white as a hospital bed sheet."

His piercing eyes made her pulse skitter. "No, thanks. I'm fine."

"Please sit. I'm sure it would make not only me, but you feel better." He edged the chair toward her. He removed his sunglasses from his head and hooked one arm of the glasses frame in the pocket of his shirt's breast pocket.

"Well. All right. You're right. I guess I don't feel that steady." It was hard for her to acknowledge she was more shaken than she cared to admit. "My head took a good knocking, but I'm okay."

Daisy tried to distract herself from his inquiring eyes. Leaning toward the open front door, she watched neighbors begin to mill outside the bungalow. They edged closer and closer to the front door. Some tried to climb the front stairs and peek inside but were kept back by the police. One of them, a small thin man in a dark blue suit, vest, white shirt, and blue tie aggressively tried to push by the uniformed policemen standing inside the front door.

Daisy got up from her chair. She moved quickly and stood at the bottom of the stairs leading to the second floor. The man headed for her at the stairs.

"Hey, come back here," the Lieutenant barked. The little man pushed past the Lieutenant and glanced at Daisy. With a nasty glare, he got close to the stairs. Pretending not to hear, he rushed toward her.

Jack sprinted to the stairs and grabbed him. He pulled the man to the front door. "Stay put." Jack stared at Daisy. "And what did you think you could do by blocking his way to the upstairs?"

"Well, I didn't think. But I slowed him up, didn't I." She laughed.

Jack stared at her and shook his head. "He didn't look as if he cared if he knocked you down."

Lieutenant Sullivan moved quickly to the little man at the front door. "Get out. This is a crime scene."

"Get out of my way," the man snarled. His nostrils flared. His eyes blazed. "I need some papers that are upstairs. I'll be right back," the man yelled as his glasses fell off his face. They dropped to the floor into the milk and glass while pushing by the Lieutenant.

"No, sir. You'll have to get the papers when this is no longer a crime scene. After we finish here." The lieutenant grabbed the man's arm and held on. "This house is off-limits for anyone but the police."

Bending down, the man picked up his glasses, rubbed them on his shirt, and slipped them on his nose, "When will that be?" Biting sarcasm filled his voice.

"In a few days. Now get out of here. Give your name to the policeman outside and where we can reach you. We'll need to ask you some questions."

"I'm Charles Miller. You can find me at Paramount Pictures." He didn't try to hide his annoyance.

Jack followed him to make sure he left.

On the stairs, the man placed his hands belligerently on his hips. "I'll tell you anything you want to know," he turned and yelled over his shoulder as he left. "I have no secrets."

The Lieutenant walked to the front door, joined Jack, and looked out at the lawn. When he saw the coroner back his black van up and drive it close to the front door, he shouted. "The coroner is here. Let the photographer and Medical Examiner get by, people. Move." He saw the men jump out of the van and open the back doors; he turned to one of his officers. "Escort the crowd gathering close to the house far away from the sidewalk to the front door. Get them on the grass."

"Wait just a minute. Is the person here who made the phone call to the police?"

The coroner and his assistant moved into the house and waited for the Lieutenant to finish interviewing the neighbor.

A heavyset woman slowly stepped forward and walked toward the front doorway. She stood near Jack. "It...It was me...me," she stammered. "I live next door." The woman wore baggy, brown slacks and teal sweater. She had a small, plaid woolen blanket around her shoulders. Daisy moved closer to the woman and listened.

"All right. What did you see? The rest of you people move. Tell me precisely what you saw." Lieutenant Sullivan stood next to the neighbor.

"My husband and I are neighbors. Last night I thought I heard a car backfiring. I went to the window." She lit the cigarette she held in her hand. "Someone, a man, walked from Mr. Walsh's house. He didn't run. He took his time. I forgot about it." She hesitated. "When I heard the scream a little while ago, I knew something was very wrong. What I heard last night must have been a gunshot, not a car backfiring. I called you right away." Her voice was gravelly, like someone who had too many cigarettes and alcohol.

"Are you sure it was a man?" the Lieutenant asked.

"Well, the person was dressed in a long, dark coat. A dark scarf was pulled high on his neck, covering his face, and a fedora pulled low over his forehead. But...He did swish as he walked. He or she looked into my window, right at me, and didn't hurry. Now, I'm confused. I'm not sure if it was a man," she whispered — her hand on her breast.

"What time did you see the person?"

"Let's see." She took a long drag on her cigarette and blew smoke rings. "We finished dinner. I cleaned up. Then we sat down to listen to the radio. It...it was about 7:30. The Lone Ranger radio program came on."

"All right, thank you. If you think of anything else, call me at the station." Detective Donovan reached into his pocket, pulled out his card, and handed it to her.

"I will." She flicked the ash at the end of the cigarette onto the sidewalk.

Daisy moved to the door and looked at the front lawn, and the newspaper reporters tripping over each other to get to the woman walking away from the house. The winner was a young man with red hair and freckles. He knew just how to slip through a crowd to get his interview. His raincoat picked up behind him. It seemed to be helping him fly to the woman. He held up a pad of paper and a pen.

"What's your name?" he asked loudly.

"Betsy Maclean." She beamed from ear to ear.

"Will you spell your last name? Please."

"Capital M small letters a c l e a n."

Daisy listened as another neighbor, a man, approached the police and started to talk.

She smiled. *Well, she's getting her moment of fame. She'll see her name in all the LA papers. Now he wants to get his name in the print.*

"Lieutenant, Lieutenant. I thought I heard a car backfiring. It must have been a gunshot. Then I heard a car engine. It came from behind the gazebo." Smiling, he looked pleased when a reporter rushed to his side and started another interview.

Lieutenant Sullivan motioned to the crowd and yelled. "If anybody has anything to add, give your statements to a uniformed policeman."

Daisy watched the group of neighbors on the lawn in front of 4B. No one else came forward to volunteer information.

The Lieutenant barked again at the policeman. "Make sure no more neighbors have anything to add. If they do, take their statements. When you're finished, get all the bystanders out of here and get the yellow tape from my patrol car. Put it over the terrace doors. When we finish here, string it across the front door."

Daisy backed away from   the doorway of 4B. She watched the coroner holding a small black bag, and a photographer with a leather strap attached to his camera swung over his shoulder rush up the front stairs. The men pushed stragglers, still on the top step of the porch, out of the way as they entered through the doorway.

Following them, Daisy moved back into the room near the dead body. She stared at the photographer snapping pictures. The flashes of light and cracking of the flashbulbs with each photo filled the air. The camera's shudder clicks bounced off the walls.

The Coroner bent down and studied the body. "Well, what do we have here?" He turned toward Jack Donovan. "Victim, male. About fifty years of age. Shot with a small-caliber gun, probably a .38, in the back. He lost a lot of blood. The bullet must have hit a major artery. Most likely died immediately. Some of the blood splattered on the table in front of him and the chairs before he fell. Most of it is under the body," he said, turning the body to its side. He studied it for a moment. "Fully dressed. Dead about twelve hours."

The lieutenant glanced at his watch. "That fits with the time the neighbor said she heard backfiring of a car and now thinks it was a gunshot. She saw the person leaving the house and walking away toward the street in front of the gazebo at about 7:30," the lieutenant said. "Anything else?"

"I'll be able to tell you more after I do an autopsy." He turned to the photographer. "All done?"

The photographer nodded.

"Let's remove the body."

Everyone stood quietly until Desmond Cunningham Walsh was placed in a black body bag, loaded on a stretcher, situated in the coroner's wagon, and the wagon pulled away from the home.

Daisy watched the valet. He seemed to be getting more and more agitated. His eyes never moved from the bloodied floor where the body of his employer vacated. He twisted his hands and had difficulty making eye contact with the police. Drops of water dripped down his cheeks—lines of tension formed in his brow.

"How long did you work for Mr. Walsh, Mr. Peavey?"

"A…about s…six months," Peavey stammered. "I only work days and early evenings. Last night, I left after dinner."

"Was there anyone else at the house when you left?"

"Y…yes. Mabel Vidor. She was going to be one of the stars in his next movie. At least that's what he told her. He really had someone else in mind. I made them drinks, martinis." His eyes grew large. "I guess I shouldn't have said that. Even though it's Prohibition, Mr. Walsh could always get alcohol. He liked his martinis. After I made the drinks, he dismissed me for the rest of the evening."

"Who worked here before you? Do you know why he left his job?"

"I think, I think his name was Harry Pryor? Not sure why he left. Mr. Walsh didn't gossip. However, I got the idea the man was dishonest. There were times when Mr. Walsh hinted the man stole money and wrote bad checks."

"I think you should come to the station."

"But, I'm innocent. You can't arrest me. This lady was lying on the floor when I entered the house." He pointed to Daisy. "She may have killed him."

"I'm telling you the truth," Daisy raised her voice when she spoke. "He was dead when I came into the house. Someone knocked me down while I stood at the body deciding what to do. Whoever it was, rushed by me, pushed me, and ran out of the terrace doors before I lost consciousness. My head hit the wall. That man..." She pointed to Peavey. "He was standing in the room, screaming when I came around. I have a lump on the back of my head to prove I got knocked out." Daisy rubbed the back of her head.

"Neither of you are under arrest. I'm sure both of you are innocent. Try to relax, Mr. Peavey. Come with me to the station. You may be able to remember more away from the scene of the murder. Jack, you stay here and look around. Take Miss O'Malley to the hospital and have her checked out when you finish here." The lieutenant frowned. "I'm going to leave some men to get fingerprints."

"I'm fine. Please don't worry about me." She began to feel dizzy. Not wanting Jack Donovan to see how she felt, she walked around the desk and sat down quickly under the photo of President Hardy.

Jack stood with his hands in his pockets.

"You're not all right." Jack walked to her and gently pushed a stray tendril of her reddish-gold hair away from her cheek. His eyes were sharp and assessing. Staring into her green eyes, he pulled the escaping tendrils of her hair behind her ear. "You stay here while I look around. I'm going to take a quick look and will only be a minute." He smiled.

Her eyes met his. She felt a shock run through her from his touch. Daisy watched him unbutton the cuffs of his shirt and roll up his sleeves. Her pulse quickened. Meeting his warm smile, she wasn't able to miss his commanding air of self-confidence and how he moved with grace. The wind and sun bronzed his face and arms. There was restless energy about his movements.

I'm sure it's not just me. His captivating presence would make any woman's heart beat a little faster. Daisy smiled. Her heart hadn't slowed down since she first saw him. She felt warmth creep from her chest to her cheeks. He totally captured her attention. *It could never be. I come from 2018.*

She felt a cool breeze and turned, looking around the room and thought she saw the dead man.

He stood beside her chair at the desk. Putting his index finger to his lips, he whispered, "Quiet."

Showing himself to me must mean he needs my help to find out what happened. I guess now I'm not only able to slip back in time, but my ability to see apparitions is back. He needs my help to prove who murdered him.

"Wait. I don't need to go to the hospital. I'm coming with you. I'm fine now, really. I just got up too fast before. That made me feel a little dizzy." Her voice was firm. Daisy was determined to see what she could find out about the dead man and why someone murdered him. Showing no sign of relenting, she stood. Her back stiffened.

Daisy watched Jack stared at her. She immediately realized he knew she was strong-minded and determined to search with him.

"You are going to have trouble getting rid of me. You don't want me to get into a problem if I investigate on my own do you? She smiled when she heard him sigh and saw him pull two pairs of latex gloves from his pocket and hand one pair to her.

Her smile grew when she heard him say, "All right, two sets of eyes are better than one, or in this case, four eyes are better than two." He laughed. "Right after a quick look, we're going to the hospital and no argument."

Daisy smiled. She knew he wasn't convinced she would be a help, but he didn't insist she stay in the chair until he finished his investigation. She would have to prove she could be of help.

CHAPTER THREE

The motive doesn't seem to be burglary. Did you notice the diamond ring he was wearing?" Daisy asked.

"Yes. He also had on a watch that looked like it was platinum."

Daisy moved to the desk. She looked down at the open checkbook and drummed her fingers on the desk pad. "According to this, he withdrew three thousand dollars two days ago." She held up the checkbook. Squinting, she flipped through the pages. He withdrew large sums of money every once in a while. Pulling open the top drawer of the desk, she moved around the papers. "Well, well, guess what I just found."

"What?"

"A stack of money. Right next to a silver cigarette case." She picked up the bills and started to count. "One thousand. It's all in hundreds. Two thousand, three thousand dollars. That seems to be the three thousand he withdrew. He didn't have time to spend it or give it to the person it was meant for."

"See any drugs in the desk drawers?"

She opened all the drawers and pushed around the contents of each one. "No."

"Anything interesting?"

"Just a bunch of keys." She held them up. "That's interesting. Each key has a tape with initials." She looked closely at them. "Most of the keys have a letter M on the tape stuck to them. I wonder how he told them apart. I would be willing to bet none of them fit any of the locks here in this house." She moved aside some more papers. "Nothing else of interest."

"What are those papers on top of the desk?"

"He was doing his 1921 taxes. He earned thirty-eight thousand dollars last year." She glanced at the other papers. "There are some news articles about WWI, description of battles, and pictures of soldiers. Here's a paper." She held it up and looked closer. "Looks like it's a list of some of the things in the home. There's a description of everything and their value. Lots of his furniture seems to be antiques. Maybe the list is for insurance purposes."

"Nothing here to question, except the money. Let's go upstairs." Jack said. "Put everything together, and I'll see it all gets to the station."

Daisy walked past Jack, hurrying out of the room to the hall and staircase leading to the second floor. Her feet tapped lightly on the steps as she ran to the second floor. She stopped and stood in the doorway of the bedroom at the top of the stairs on the right.

"This must be his room. He had good taste." She stared at the bed covered in a taupe duvet and wingback chairs covered in the same material. Curtains in a dark brown, shiny material covered the tall windows. The carpet was off white.

"Look at these." She walked over to a long, rich, dark wooden dresser and picked up a pile of letters tied together with everyday string, sitting on the top. Untying the stack, she opened the first envelope and slid out a letter. She ran it under her nose. "Hmmm. Perfumed. It smells like lilies." She began to read.

"What does it say?"

Dear Desmond,
My time with you last night was wonderful. I hated to leave you. I can honestly say I'm falling in love with you. I hope we can marry soon. We will have a wonderful life.
Love, M

Daisy smiled. Replacing the letter, she pulled another from the next envelope.

Jack opened the drawers of the bedside table. "Nothing here. What do the other letters say?" Jack asked. He watched Daisy open several envelopes and read them.

"They're all love letters. It looks as if they are from different women. The writing is not the same on all of them, but all are signed with an *M*. A couple of them discuss the possibility of marriage."

"He was quite a lover," Jack chuckled. "Haven't found any drugs in the dresser drawers." He walked to the other side of the bed and searched the nightstand. "No letters here, but look at this, a police report."

He pulled out a single page. "It's made out for a Harry Pryor. He listed his place of employment as valet at 4B South Alvardaro Drive in Hollywood. The date he left employment was six months ago. The report listed the reason for his dismissal was theft. By the date, it looks as if he was the valet before Peavey. I don't see in this report that Walsh wanted the police to arrest Pryor. He just wanted to make a report to have on record with the police. However, he did fire him."

"We'll see what Peavey had to say when we get to the station."

He ran his hand around the drawer. "What do we have here?" He bent down and reached to the back of the drawer.

"What did you find?"

He slid out a gold locket tucked in the corner of the bedside table and dangled it so that Daisy could see it.

She took it and opened it. "Photos. A blonde woman on one side. She squinted and looked at the other picture. "It's a picture of the murdered man."

She stared at it.

He walked to her, took back the locket, and placed it next to the letters.

"Do you think the Lieutenant has gotten a list of Walsh's friends from Peavey?"

"If I know the Lieutenant, he got the list from Peavey and more information. We'll find out when we get to the station."

Daisy turned toward the closet, grabbed the doorknob, and twisted it. The door easily swung open. "I see four men's suits and several shirts." He wasn't a clothes horse though; they are all in the latest style. There are four pairs of shoes with trees on the floor. "Wait, next to them is a handkerchief." She bent down and picked it up. "There's the letter M embroidered in the corner."

She pushed the hangers to the side. "Look at this." She pulled out a shear, pink silk nightgown hanging from a hook on the back wall of the closet. "It also has an embroidered M." She slipped the gown from the hook and held it up to her so that Jack could see. "What do you think?"

Jack laughed. "Not your size."

"Too big." She smiled. "It looks as if someone was trying to hide it." She folded the gown and handkerchief and laid them next to the letters.

"Did you notice the framed photos of actresses on Walsh's walls in the room with the desk?" Daisy asked. "They were all signed. Most of them were of women with blonde hair, except for Charlotte Miles. I think I remember, from her picture in the room where he was murdered, she's a brunette."

"Yes. I bet some of the women in photos hanging on the walls wrote the letters."

"I'm sure of it. A lot of the women have M for the first initial of their first names."

"Well, that's interesting. We have to check all the women whose first names start with M when we get back to the police station." Daisy smiled. "In the photographs downstairs, there are three women with the initial M in their first name, but I would bet only one woman belongs to the locket, handkerchief, and nightgown."

"What's in the room next door?"

Daisy slid out of the room and into the room across the hall. "Another bedroom." She started a search, opening the drawers of the bureau, bedside table, and the closet. "They're all empty. Must be a guest room. "Here's a photo of a not-too-attractive young girl. No name. I wonder who she is. Maybe his daughter."

"How about the bathroom?" Jack slid into the bathroom at the end of the hall.

Daisy waited in the doorway and watched as he checked the mirrored medicine chest.

"Only the usual razor, soap, comb and brush, and toothbrush and paste. No drugs." He drew his lips in thoughtfully. "Okay. Guess we're finished. Let's go."

"Next stop, the police station." Daisy smiled. She ran down the stairs.

"Did you forget your hospital visit? That's our next stop."

"No. I didn't forget the hospital, though I think it's a waste of time. I'll go, but I'm interested in this case and want to help. Let's get it over with. I hope the stop at the hospital won't take long." Daisy smiled. "Where's your car?" she asked, walking toward the front door.

"My patrol car is right in the front."

He nodded to the police checking for fingerprints on the first floor as he passed the room where the body was found. "There's some letters, locket and nightgown and handkerchief upstairs in the bedroom at the top of the stairs. Bring them with you and the things from the desk when you come back to the station."

Daisy threw open the front door and was greeted by yellow tape that bounced like a rubber band when she hit it. Laughing, she ducked under and waited until Jack joined her. She followed him down the sidewalk to his car. *I want to get this hospital visit over with.*

Daisy opened the car door. "I want to start on the investigation."

"Slide in." Jack slammed shut the passenger door and ignored her. He jumped into his side of the parked car, pushed the key into the ignition, and revved the motor. "All right, we'll stop at the police headquarters after you get checked out."

"You can go. There's no traffic coming."

"You're in a hurry. Suppose someone was crossing the street."

"I looked. No one was there."

He laughed. "All right, I'm going."

"I'm in a hurry." She watched him drive on the gravel road and slowly pull onto the main street into traffic.

Daisy stared out of the window as they drove. People walking on the sidewalks darted in and out of stores and office buildings. She smiled. *The men look as if they are going to a funeral, wearing black suits, white shirts, hats, and ties. The women are in dark dresses — no shorts and flip-flops. The cars, Model T Fords, are black. A trolley is running in the middle of the road, separating the one-way streets: one going south and one going north.* "It's a beautiful day." She rolled down the window and coughed. Quickly rolling the window up, she coughed again. "The gas fumes are unpleasant."

A large gray stone building with a circular drive came into view on the right. Bethany Hospital was printed in large black letters on the front of the building.

"Here we are." Jack drove off the main road and turned into the driveway. He slid into a parking space next to the door of the Emergency Room. She wondered how medicine was administered in 1922. *Not great, she bet. So much has been discovered since 1922.*

"I hope this won't take very long."

"Wait right here. I'll get a nurse."

Before the Emergency Room door slipped closed, she heard a woman's voice and assumed it belonged to a nurse. "You here again?"

"It's not me this time. It's my friend. She was pushed by a burglar. Fell and hit her head. Unconscious for a few minutes." The doors of the emergency room closed with a thud. Disappointed, Daisy was unable to hear any more of the conversation. She waited patiently.

When the doors opened again, a portly woman with gray hair pulled in a knot at the back of her neck stepped into the parking lot. She wore a white uniform and cap. A thin black, velvet band ran across the front of the hat. Her stockings and low, laced shoes were white. Walking beside Jack, she pushed a wheelchair toward the patrol car.

"Do you really think a wheelchair is necessary?" Daisy asked, opening the passenger door. She leaned toward the nurse, hoping to find an ally. It didn't happen.

"Yes, dear. Everyone comes into and leaves the hospital in a wheelchair. It's a rule." The nurse pulled the chair near Daisy and patted the seat with a substantial hand.

"All right." Daisy knew better than argue with someone in authority—no doubt this nurse was in charge. She had to cooperate and didn't want Jack to think she wasn't grateful he wanted to make sure she was okay. Most of all, she wanted to collaborate to make sure he would let her keep helping on the case. Daisy sprang out of the car and dropped into the wheelchair. Not trusting herself to show her irritation, she pressed her lips tightly together, so no sound escaped.

"Just let them examine you to make sure you're okay." Jack patted her shoulder as he walked beside her into the emergency room.

The nurse pushed Daisy past a desk where several nurses, without black stripes on their caps, stood. *The stripe might mean she's in charge.* She watched them look up and wave to Jack.

"You must be here frequently." Daisy looked up at Jack.

"He is, dear." The nurse laughed. "He certainly is."

The chair hummed as it rolled over a black linoleum floor. Well past the desk, the nurse stopped at a cubical surrounded by a white curtain and pushed Daisy into the space. A bed with a white gown on the pillow sat next to a blood pressure machine. A paper bag laid on the sheet at the end of the bed. "Change into the gown and put your clothes into this bag. You can keep on your underthings." She handed Daisy a large paper bag. "Keep the gown's ties in front."

Jack waved. His brows drew together when his eyes met hers. "I'll be right here," he said as the nurse closed the curtain.

Daisy turned and gave Jack a little wave just as the nurse finished closing the curtain. "I'm okay. Don't worry."

The nurse looked at Jack. "You can stay in the waiting room. You know where it is. I'll come and get you when we're finished." She looked over her shoulder, waving him down the hall to her right. She turned to Daisy. "He's usually the patient."

* * * *

While walking to the room the nurse had pointed out, a flicker of apprehension flowed through Jack. He flopped down on a two-seater, tan leather couch and picked up a magazine from the table in front of him. He flipped through the pages without really seeing the content. He clenched his teeth. He hardly knew Daisy, but he was worried. Head injuries could be severe. He needed to hear she was all right, and then he could relax. He felt a connection to her as soon as he saw her sparkling green eyes and luxurious, lustrous, long auburn hair that hung below her shoulders. An unusual style for today, he thought. Most women have short bobs. The iron determination of her chin made him smile. She seemed to have a strength that didn't lessen her femininity.

* * * *

In an hour, the scraping of opening curtains echoed through the emergency room. Daisy felt good. The doctor said she was okay. The nurse pushed Daisy's wheelchair to the waiting room. "Okay, Detective, she's finished."

Jack looked up. Daisy was dressed in her boots, blood-soaked jeans, and sweater. "Thank goodness. I finished all the magazines and the afternoon edition of the newspaper. The story of the murder is on the front page." He tossed the magazine in his hand onto the table. Picking up the newspaper, he handed it to Daisy. "The murder managed to make the late afternoon paper."

She stared at the bold headlines and began to read the story on the front page of the Hollywood Edition of the Los Angeles, California newspaper as the nurse pushed her wheelchair toward the exit.

Death of Famous Director

January 2, 1922. Afternoon edition of the Los Angeles news.

Hollywood still celebrating the New Year while a famous director murdered.

Desmond Cunningham Walsh, fifty-two years old, famous in the film industry, was murdered in his home on New Year's Eve. He lived alone in an upscale neighborhood with homes owned by the Hollywood elite. He was born William Deane Taylor in County Carlow, Ireland, but changed his name to Desmond Cunningham Walsh when he entered in the United States at Ellis Island.

He studied drama at Marlborough College in England and hoped to further a career in theater in New York City.

Walsh took time out to marry Ethel May Woodson of the prominent New York City Woodson family. They opened an antique shop and became well-known members of New York City society.

On October 23, 1908, he disappeared from New York City. Abandoning his family, he crossed the border into Canada and took time out to fight in World War I with a Canadian army unit. After the war, he traveled with a group of actors around Canada and the United States. He worked at various acting jobs in small theaters.

When he passed through the Fantasy Land gates of Tinsel Town in 1912, he entered into a town of wealth and glamour. Desiring to escape the gloom of World War I, he joined those who broke with Victorian morals. He attached himself to groups that fought for the women's rights to vote, enjoyed ragtime, jazz, and blues music. He patronized speakeasies and enjoyed homebrewed liquor. He was not one to avoid the strictures of prohibition.

Walsh helped with the investigation of the rise of organized crime in Hollywood and worked with the assistant United Stated Attorney to eradicate drugs in the movie industry. Until the last day of 1921, he managed to survive the seamy side of Hollywood and did not allow it to chew him up and leave him in misery.

He acted in several silent movies and became incredibly successful as a director of Silent Films. Directing his first film in 1914, he had over sixty films to his credit. He was about to start on a silent film featuring Mary Pickford, a well-known star of our time and sought after by all directors.

He reconciled with his family a short time before his death and is survived by a daughter, Helen.

The funeral will be held on January 4th in Oakley Cemetery at eleven o'clock.

Daisy handed the newspaper to Jack. "He was an important man."

"Here, let me have that." The nurse took the paper from Jack and tucked the paper under her arm.

Jack walked beside her wheelchair. "Is the patient all right?"

"She's fine. She'll have a lump on her head for a while, but everything else is fine. I'll let her tell you. She can resume all activities."

"The doctor gave me a clean bill of health." Daisy looked upward, nodded, and smiled at him. "I told you I was all right."

The nurse pushed Daisy's wheelchair to the exit of the emergency room. "Your last ride today." The nurse smiled. "I hope, unless you get mixed up in any more of the Detective's antics."

As they passed the nurses station, the two young nurses standing behind the desk smiled at Jack.

"Call me." One of them said, hurrying to the front of the desk. "Haven't changed my home phone number and the extension here is the same." She winked.

Daisy felt a twinge in her stomach. Puzzled, she bit her lip and looked away. Her thoughts scampered quickly around. She was puzzled. She sighed and then smiled. The tense lines in her face relaxed.

"Send the bill to the police department," he called over his shoulder, ignoring the girl.

Daisy sighed again, but this time with relief. "I forgot about a bill." *My medical insurance wouldn't cover me in 1922.* "Thank you so much." She looked at Jack.

He leaned toward her and stared into her eyes. "Tell me. Are you sure the doctor said you're okay?"

"It's what the nurse said. The lump on the back of my head will be around for a while. I also have a mild concussion, but no broken bones, cracked ribs, or skull fracture. I had x-rays. The doctor said I might have a lingering headache. Haven't had one yet." *Thank goodness I didn't have open wounds. Penicillin hasn't been invented yet to fight off infection or broken bones. I don't need an amputation of any limb.* A stubborn line set her chin. Her arms crossed over her chest.

He patted her shoulder and helped her out of the wheelchair. "I'm sure he told you to be careful and rest."

She smiled. Her heart danced with excitement. *Why am I getting these reactions? I'm not from the 1920s. Nothing can happen between us. But I'm here now, and I'm going to help solve this murder.*

She waved to the nurse. Sliding into the front passenger seat, she closed the car door and waited for Jack to start the motor. "He didn't say anything of the kind. There are no restrictions. I can help with the case."

"She was quiet and twisted her earring several minutes on the drive to the police station.

When they reached a large brick building, Jack pulled into a space in front of the building. "Come on. This is the police station." He left the driver's seat, opened her door, and led her to the front steps. "Let's see what Sullivan has found out."

Feeling dizzy, she grabbed his arm.

"Are you all right?" He slid his arm around her waist and pulled her to him. "You aren't. You're dizzy, aren't you?"

"I'm all right. I just got out of the car too fast. I'm not confused, have nausea, or blurred vision. So, I must be okay." She found his nearness exciting. The tenderness in his gaze brought a smile to her face. *Stop. Enough is enough. I'm only here because of some freak accident sending me into 1922. I could be in Victorian times. A place I would like to be. But, Fate brought me to1922, and I'll make the best of it.*

She had to take two steps to his one as he led her to the front staircase, then to a reception room where a Sergeant sat at a marred wooden desk. The hardwood floor was scratched and dusty. Two teenagers sat, handcuffed next to a uniformed policeman. At the end of the room, a young woman sat on a bench and sang a sad tune. She was answering the questions, with a pencil, on the paper in her lap.

"He's waiting for you, Detective."

Jack pulled open the door leading into a large room with a well-worn, coffee-stained olive green carpet. Smoke bellowed into the entrance door.

She watched the men who smoked, lighting their next cigarette on the previous one before they rubbed it out. Daisy glanced around the room, packed with army green, metal filing cabinets, and old scratched wooden desks. Ashtrays filled with ashes, stubbed out cigarettes or cigars, ringing phones, lots of papers, manila folders, and envelopes laid haphazardly on top of them. Narrow, rectangular dirty windows were near the ceiling that appeared never opened. Voices boomed off the walls of the smoke-filled room where Jack led her to the back. A weathered door, with a glass window, was closed. Underneath "Lieutenant

Detective" was the name, Enzo Sullivan, each line painted in bold, black ink.

Jack knocked, turned the door handle, and motioned for Daisy to follow him into the office.

She looked around upon entering. The office was a miniature of the outer room, except for a large open window in the middle of the exterior wall. The room hadn't been cleaned in this century. Thick dust covered the sill. Next to a pile of papers on the lone desk, a large cigar dangled on the edge of a metal ashtray. Smoke curled from the stogie and floated toward the open window. A half-eaten hamburger sat on a plate, in a pool of catsup, next to the cigar. The walls, plastered with public information posters, papers, and "wanted" posters, had chips of green paint missing on the wall from removed tape or furniture hitting them.

"How are you, Daisy? The Lieutenant bellowed as he tossed an envelope on the pile of papers at the corner of his desk.

"I'm good, really. Passed my x-rays and exam with flying colors."

The lieutenant tipped back his chair and stared at her. "Have a seat. How are you, really?" The Lieutenant took the papers in front of him and stuffed them into a manila envelope on his lap. "What's with the bandage on your forehead?" He leaned forward. The chair landed on all four legs with a loud crash.

She pushed her hair behind an ear and twisted her earring. "I'm fine. Believe me."

"Were you hiding something from me?" Jack asked. He leaned forward and stared at her.

"Just a little scratch. A superficial cut. The doctor put a bandage on it so the dirt would stay out, and it wouldn't get infected." She looked at him. "I probably can take it off now." She peeled it off.

"There's a wastebasket on the side of the desk."

"Thanks." She bent over and dropped it into the basket. *There's not even any blood on the bandage — a good sign.*

Raising her head, she studied the Lieutenant. He appeared tired and untidy—loose tie and wrinkled shirt. She noticed large sweat stains under his arms when he reached for the cigar. He inhaled deeply. Exhaling, he blew smoke rings.

"Where is the valet Peavey?" Jack asked.

CHAPTER FOUR

We had to let him go. With the statement you gave us, Daisy, and with what he said about his arrival at the home, we couldn't hold him. He didn't commit the murder. Before Peavey left, he gave us a lot of information. He gave us a list of Walsh's closest friends and the people he worked with." He lifted a manila envelope from the pile of papers. "He also opened and told us more about the valet before him."

"At the house, we found a police report for Harry Pryor in the bedside table. Walsh filed a report on him but dropped the charges. The police at the house will bring everything we found when they return," Jack reported. "Walsh didn't press charges. Nobody knows why. When he didn't give a reason, the police didn't pursue the incident. The report is with the other papers from the house."

"We had Peavey identify the body. It sent him into a tizzy. I thought we were going to have another patient on our hands, someone else we would have to take to the hospital. He almost fainted." Sullivan shook his head.

"Before he left, he said a young woman visited Walsh two weeks ago, and he heard them having quite an argument. He didn't know who she was or her name. Walsh didn't tell him anything about her or the argument."

"Maybe one of his friends knows who she was? Do we know where the previous valet is?" Jack asked.

"Seems that Pryor was left in charge when Walsh went on vacation for a week. When he returned, Pryor was gone but not before forging checks and cashing them. He stole jewelry and Walsh's car. The vehicle was the only thing returned before Pryor left the area. The police found the car near the gazebo a few days after Walsh got back. Now, no one can find Pryor. He has simply disappeared."

"Did you get an address for him?" Daisy asked.

"Nope. The last time seen, he was driving over the US border into Canada in another stolen car."

A knock on the door interrupted the conversation.

"Come in."

A patrolman in a uniform handed the lieutenant a slip of paper and a bag. He left quickly.

"Thanks." The lieutenant opened the bag and looked over the contents.

"Those are the things we found at the house."

"Please, get them to the evidence room." He handed the bag to Jack. "The paper is a telegraphed report from the Canadians. The border patrol who reported Pryor going into Canada sent it. Pryor was wanted on a burglary charge in Buffalo, New York before he escaped into Canada."

"What's in the report?"

"The report says the Mounties searched the wilds of Canada, but he's not been found and they listed him as deceased."

Probably is, thought Daisy.

"Listen, Jack." Sullivan searched through the pile of papers on his desk. He handed a manila file to Jack. "Most of Walsh's friends were women and connected with the film industry. A woman and actress would be able to get information from them that you may not be able to get." He stared at Jack. "I've decided to let Miss O'Malley go with you to the interviews. She'll be a big help. You know how actresses can be." He turned and winked at Daisy.

I have the Lieutenant Detective's okay. She put the comment out of her mind. *Was what he said an insult?* She wanted to be part of the investigation and said nothing. *Jack let me investigate things at the bungalow. Now I'm officially part of the murder case, so who cares if he meant something uncomplimentary.*

"Chief," Jack roared. "I let Daisy help at the house, but I didn't think she would be helping with the whole case." Annoyance crossed his face along with gritted teeth.

Sullivan raised his hand. "I've made the decision, she helps." His voice was firm and final.

Daisy's heart sank when she heard the tone of Jack's voice. She watched him warily as he cleared his throat and started to protest again. Her eyes met his sidelong glance. He studied her for a moment and turned away. He used a tone when he spoke that she had not heard since she met him.

He sighed with exasperation. "All right, as long as Miss O'Malley is careful and follows my orders." His voice was resigned, and he shrugged. Matter-of-factly, he picked up the manila envelope and turned to her. "Look this over." He pushed the manila folder into her hands.

Daisy smiled sweetly and took the file. She bit her lip, determined not to show her joy.

"Did the coroner have any more info when he did the autopsy?" Daisy asked.

"Don't know. Hasn't sent me anything," the Lieutenant said, smiling at Daisy. The phone rang. He grabbed the receiver, leaned into the phone, and listened. "Yea! Okay, will send them down." He slipped the receiver back in its cradle. "Ask, and you shall receive. The coroner has some results."

"Come with me." Jack turned to Daisy. "We're going to the morgue." He waved to the chief, hurried Daisy out of the office, and pulled her to the stairs. He threw open the door, grabbed her arm, and dragged her through it before it swung closed and hit her. She followed as he ran down the flight of stairs.

"Let me carry that before you drop it." His tone was formal. He stuck out his hand.

She handed him the folder. "Thank you."

Running to the lower floor, she noticed the temperature cooled. Daisy wrapped her arms around herself. Out of breath and hoping not to fall, she watched her feet as she ran. At the end of the staircase and on the flat floor, she stood and gazed out a large window covered with a curtain to her left. The cold of the gray cement floor seeped into her shoes. The dim fluorescent light of the hallway cast shadows on the wall.

A cold blast of air hit when Jack pushed open the morgue door. She stared at a white tiled floor splattered with blood, as was the coroner's lab coat that hung on a hook inside the door. Blood also splattered the blue scrub suit the coroner wore. She stopped and scanned the room. She saw a large sink against the wall. A long hose attached to the faucet stretched to a drain in the middle of the floor. A row of metal doors along the back wall were closed, except one opened to an empty space. A body covered with a sheet laid on a stretcher near the middle of the floor. A scale hung from the ceiling over a table next to the body. Jars with organs lined a shelf.

"Hi there. You're just in time," the coroner glanced at them. "I just finished and was beginning to record my report."

"What did you find?" Jack asked.

Daisy watched the coroner pull back the sheet. A soft gasp escaped her.

"Are you okay?" Jack asked.

She noticed a thawing in his voice. "I'm fine." Standing away from the body, she clasped her arms around herself. "Just a little cold."

The Y-shaped incision ran straight from the shoulders to the pubic area. Even though sewn up, it still gave her the creeps. The closed eyes, if they had been open, would have been cloudy and staring at the ceiling.

"Well, the bullet entered the right side of the spine, low in the torso, and went upward. It lodged in the left breast. The bullet hole in his coat over his heart didn't correspond with the one in his chest. He must have been standing with his arms up. He was probably taken by surprise by someone hiding in the house and was threatened by the killer."

Jack turned to Daisy. "Might have been someone who entered when he left the house to say goodbye to his female guest and valet. Maybe he was surprised and raised his hands in the air."

He looked back at the coroner. "Is there anything else?" Jack looked at the body.

"The gun was a .38-caliber revolver. The bullet is with his clothes. I found two blond hairs under the collar of his jacket. Nothing under his nails. That's about it." He handed Jack an envelope holding the hairs, the clothes, and bullet. "I'll send a written report to the Lieutenant."

"Thanks." Jack tucked the bag under his arm with the file he held.

"Come on, Daisy. These items will be in storage until the trial is over," he said. "I have to go to the clerk's office. He checks everything in and stores them in the evidence room. He's at the end of the hall. We'll stop at Sullivan's office before we leave." He guided her out of the morgue and to the door at the end of the hall. "Wait here. It will only take me a minute." He pushed open the door.

The door remained ajar, allowing Daisy to overhear the conversation.

"Hi, George. Got some things for you. They're from the Walsh case."

"They'll be safe here."

"See you at trial time."

The door swung closed and Daisy heard no more. She looked around at the gray stone walls and shivered. "I would never want to work down here," she whispered while waiting for Jack.

"I'm back. Let's go."

She smiled. His voice had warmed.

A blanket of smoke hit her, and her eyes burned when the door to the squad room opened. Walking across the large room, she heard a male voice yelling at the Lieutenant Detective.

"Why did the police pick me up? I've done nothing wrong. I have work to do, movies and films."

"And just what do you do, Mr. Miller?"

"I told you I'm at Paramount Pictures."

Without knocking, Jack opened the door and entered the office. Daisy stood beside him.

The lieutenant turned to Jack and Daisy. "I'm having a conversation with Mr. Charles Miller." He turned to the man sitting in front of his desk. "I asked you a question, Mr. Miller, and you didn't answer me. What exactly is your position there?"

"I'm a film producer and director at Paramount Pictures. I'm a big deal there. I also represent some of the actors."

Jack and Daisy watched the interrogation with interest.

"Why did you insist on going upstairs at Walsh's house?" Jack asked.

"I needed some papers Desmond was keeping."

"What were the exact papers you wanted?" Sullivan asked.

"There were some letters to him from a lady I know. And some papers I needed for a meeting.

Walsh does or did, some work with the Attorney General on drugs in Hollywood and the film industry, as do I. We were going to have a meeting in Los Angeles. He couldn't attend the meeting, and I needed any information he found. I also needed some contracts and papers I believed Walsh had."

"Did you find contracts or papers belonging to this gentleman when you searched the upstairs, Jack?" He glanced at Jack and Daisy.

"No," Jack answered.

"Since I wasn't allowed upstairs and you didn't find them, I guess they were already with the commission. The meeting was called off because of Walsh's murder."

"I work with many of the women Desmond worked with. Why don't you keep your questions for Mable Vidor and others?" Miller asked.

"Why? Do you know something about his lady friends and what their names are?" Daisy asked.

"Tell us about some of these people." Jack opened the folder. "Mable Vidor."

"Well, I don't want to name names, but he helped get a few of the ladies into rehab." He sighed. "Mabel has a drug problem," Miller said. "I refuse to work with her."

"What about Mary Giroux?" Jack skimmed the list from the folder.

"She's a simple little girl. Very talented, but her mother runs her. She has a younger sister with a disability. The girl plays the organ at the Picture Palace in Hollywood and Venice Beach. She doesn't get along with the sister, Mary, or her mother. The mother keeps the girl hidden, so she won't interfere with Mary's career. She lives in a home with some other disabled people. They have people who help them. They say the sister tries to sabotage Mary and plays tricks on her. The mother makes her use a different name so that she won't be connected to the family."

"I've said enough. I just know he helped many people. Some of the women he helped became his close friends. Sometimes they became too dependent on his help."

"What about your work with the Drug Commission?" Daisy asked.

"I've been with them for about six months. Desmond got me involved. Why don't you keep your questions for the people I mentioned and the others on the list you are holding? I don't want to discuss any more of these people. It's their private business."

"I understand you are involved with the Mafia?" Jack asked.

"Who told you that? How do you know that?"

"Word gets around. There are no secrets in Hollywood."

"Don't be crazy…I go to the speakeasy where the Mafia hang out. I'm helping to fight the drug problem. I told you, just as Walsh was doing. Ask the Attorney General. I'm one of the good guys."

He glared at Jack. Turning to the Lieutenant, he snarled again. "You can't keep me here."

"All right, you can go. We will be calling you again."

"If there's a next time." He stood. "You can bet I'll have a lawyer with me."

Daisy stared. His eyes were level with hers. He pushed by her, stalked out, and slammed the door.

"Well, we'll be going, Chief. We'll stop in on Mabel Vidor."

"Do you think the Mafia had Walsh murdered?" Daisy asked.

"The Mafia didn't like him, but Walsh was very visible, and this prominence would make it hard for them to get away with murder, even if they hired someone to do it. I'm not sure the Mafia has their hand in this murder."

Daisy walked toward Jack. Before she could say goodbye to the lieutenant, the door swung open. With a bang, it hit the wall. Not sparing the coat of paint, it chipped the wall when it flew back and closed.

A woman, dressed in a silk pants suit, suede shoes, and a long, narrow fur slung over her shoulder, burst into the office. Dark glasses covered her eyes, and she smoked a cigarette in a long black holder. A row of small diamonds sparkled along its side. She pushed past Daisy and dropped into the chair in front of the desk, the chair Charles Miller had left. She inhaled deeply and blew out a stream of smoke.

Daisy coughed as the smoke drifted by her.

"I'm Mabel Vidor." She slid the fur off and tossed it over the arm of the chair. "My friend, Charles Miller, stopped at my house. He told my driver the police were questioning all the friends of Desmond Walsh. And I was on the list. I came right to the station."

"Didn't you see, Miller? He was just here."

"No. He must have gone out a side door."

Daisy glanced at Jack with raised eyebrows. *She isn't telling the truth.*

Jack shook his head.

"Did he tell you how he knew about the list?"

"He heard it from the valet, Mr. Peavey, who gave you a list of Walsh's friends when he was here. I was the lady at the house having drinks with Desmond the night he was murdered."

"Tell us what you know, if anything, about his murder."

"I visited Desmond after dinner. I always walk into his house without knocking. When I arrived, he was on the phone. He was having a serious conversation. When he saw me walk into the room, he quickly hung up. He didn't say goodbye, just hung up. He didn't tell me what the call was about." She took a deep drag on her cigarette. "He looked upset, and I asked him who he was talking to. He said everything was all right and not to worry." Smoke drifted from her mouth as she spoke.

"Mr. Peavey made us our favorite martini, and then Desmond said he could go for the evening. So, Mr. Peavey grabbed his jacket and left. He was talking with my driver when I left."

"Why did you visit Mr. Walsh?"

"I needed to return a book Desmond lent me. We had a drink and discussed the book. We were very good friends, love."

"Mr. Peavey said he heard you and Walsh arguing."

"That's true. I've had a little problem with drugs, and Desmond wanted me to check into rehab. I'm in the middle of a movie and can't. We fought about it."

She smiled. "He promised me, as soon as my drug problem was under control, we would marry. We argue, but we always make up. I was his true love. I hugged him goodbye and left in my limo." She smiled. "I have to confess. I told you a little white lie. We were more than friends."

"Did anyone see you leave," Jack asked.

"I told you his valet was dismissed for the evening was outside. Desmond saw me get into my car. My driver offered Mr. Peavey a ride home since we would pass his house on the way to my home. He thanked us and jumped into the front seat. Desmond was alive when we left. He came out on the porch and waved goodbye." She pulled a handkerchief from her pocket, lowered her glasses, and patted a tear that dripped from her eye. "That means I wasn't the last to see him. Please find out who murdered him. He is or was, the love of my life."

"By the way, Miss Vidor, do you own a gun?" Sullivan asked.

"No. I hate them. I have to go now." She jumped from the chair and slung her fur around her shoulders. "If you need anything more, just call me." She sniffed and pushed the glasses on her nose.

"Before you leave, I have one more question for you," Jack said. "Do you know anything about three thousand dollars he had in his desk?"

"He offered to pay for my Rehab. I wasn't the only person in Hollywood he helped. He tried to hand me the money. That was part of what we argued about. I told him I could pay my way. Finally, he dropped the offer.

"My driver is out front. He will confirm he took me home after I left Desmond. My house is on the other side of town. I went right to sleep when I got home."

"We were just leaving, Chief. I'll check with her driver."

"He'll tell you Desmond was alive when we left." She pushed her arm through Jack's and leaned on him as they walked out of the office and down the police station steps to her limo parked at the curb.

Daisy followed closely behind them.

The driver jumped from his seat and opened the back door of the limo.

Mabel slipped into the backseat. "Tell him, Sidney…When we left, Desmond was alive," she said.

The driver closed her door and returned to the driver's seat. He closed his door and started the motor. Before he pulled into the street, he rolled down his window. "The lady is correct, Detective. Mr. Walsh even waved goodbye to us."

Jack smiled and turned to Mabel. "We won't stop until we find the murderer."

Mabel Vidor slid down her window. "Thank you, Detective." She pushed her handkerchief under her glasses and dabbed her eyes. She threw him a kiss as the limo pulled away from the curb.

"She has an airtight alibi. Even if she didn't tell the truth about when she saw and spoke to Charles Miller."

"It's late afternoon now. Why don't I take you to your hotel? You can rest, and I'll take you to dinner in a couple of hours. Where are you staying?"

Daisy thought for a moment. She had seen a sign for a hotel when she left the drug store. "The hotel is near the Walsh house. It's at the end of the street that runs in front of the gazebo. It looked like a pretty nice place with its large verandas and gardens." She was guessing, but she pretty sure what she described was like the pictures she had seen of many of the hotels in Hollywood in the 1920s.

"You can tell me at dinner if there are any new developments in the case." She smiled.

"What did you think of Mabel Vidor?" he asked as they drove.

"She's an actress and a very good one, I've heard."

"Now that I've seen her in action, she certainly is."

"Did you see her dilated pupils when she slipped her glasses down? Her nose looks as if it had been bleeding recently, too. I suspect she's still having a problem with drugs. Cocaine in particular," Daisy added.

"She's very dramatic. I wonder if she knows about the other women who thought they were going to marry Desmond Cunningham Walsh."

Daisy laughed. She saw the hotel in the distance. *I was correct. It has verandas and gardens.*

"I've had quite a day. I need some rest."

Daisy watched Jack drive to the front door of the hotel. She jumped out when he stopped. "You don't have to come in. I'll be fine." She slammed the door.

"Oh. I forgot." He pulled down the passenger window and yelled to her back when she started to run to the revolving front door of the hotel.

Daisy stopped and turned.

"Take the envelope with the notes."

She ran back and grabbed the report.

"See you at seven. Dress casual," Jack called as she ran up the hotel stairs.

CHAPTER FIVE

Daisy stood and peeked through the revolving lobby door. She watched Jack's car leave the driveway. After he turned onto the main road, she waited a few more minutes to make sure he was gone and didn't turn back to the front of the hotel to tell her something he forgot to say. She walked to the registration desk. "A room with a king-size bed, please." She turned the registration book, signed it, and turned it back to the man behind the desk.

"How long will you be with us, Miss? Do you have any luggage?"

"I'm not sure how long. Probably a week. There was a fire at my apartment. I'll have to purchase new clothes. Right now, I'm wearing clothes from the wardrobe of the movie I'm in."

"Must have been a rough scene. There's blood on them."

"Oh, no, it's dried mud."

The clerk turned to the cubby holes behind him and reached for a key. He glanced at her name. "Here's your key, Miss O'Malley. You're on the third floor in the front of the hotel. You'll have a good view of the gardens. They are beautiful now."

"Can you tell me where I can buy some clothes?"

"There's a department store on Main Street and several boutiques down the alleys off Main Street."

Daisy hurried to the elevator, pushed the button, and waited. She looked around. The floor of the reception area was large squares of marble in black and gray. A dark, gray runner held down by brass rods covered the grand circular staircase to the second floor. She could see a small part of the stairs to the third floor. They went straight up and black carpet covered the steps. Flowers in season were in large vases on top of the light, cream-colored wooden tables scattered around the lobby. The glass in the central chandelier sparkled. The elevator arrived.

When the gate was pulled open by an operator, he nodded hello. She jumped in and nodded to him. He stood ramrod straight in his navy, blue uniform. The jacket with a high collar reached to his thigh and had gold shoulder bars. His trousers and skycap were navy blue. The brass buttons and shoes were polished until they shined. His white-gloved hand pulled the safety gate and turned the crank, so the elevator moved upward.

"What floor, Miss?"

"The third, please," she said as the elevator began to climb upward. She leaned against the back wall, thinking about the murder of Desmond Cunningham Walsh. The elevator bounced when it landed on the third floor. She waited for the operator to pull open the gate.

"Thank you." A cool breeze covered her. She stepped out and turned to the right. Walking to room 313, she heard footsteps and stopped. A man in a brown suit, with a large bloodstain in the front, stared at her.

Wide-eyed, she stared back at him. Her eyebrows rose in amazement. Sliding the brass key in the lock of her room, she asked, "Who are you? What do you want?" She stared. He moved closer to her, and she saw the blood covering his chest. "Are you Desmond Walsh?"

"Look to my friends very closely. You will find out who murdered me." His voice drifted off, and he turned and walked to the opposite end of the hallway. He disappeared into the wall at the end.

"Wait. Come back. Don't leave. Tell me more." Daisy waited, but the apparition didn't reappear. She turned her key, twisted the doorknob, and pushed open the door after she heard the click. Daisy glanced around the room. *That king-size bed looks so comfortable, but there's no time now to take a nap.*

A rose and jade striped duvet covered the bed. The same colored pillows covered the top of the bed. The dresser and bedside tables were a rich, dark wood. Shiny jade fabric covered the seat of a straight chair at a table and a winged-back chair near the window. She walked to the window and pulled back rose-colored drapes. It was a gorgeous day. The man in the brown suit wandered through the gardens, turned to the front of the building, and disappeared. *The desk clerk was right. The gardens are spectacular. When I have time,*

I'm going to take a walk. Paths wove around flower gardens and fountains. A couple, with children playing at their feet, sat on a bench next to a palm tree. She strained her eyes searching for the ghost. He didn't appear again.

"What I need now is money to pay for the hotel and the clothes I need. Clothes that are in- style. Clothes that look like the 1920s. That means I have to get back to my time to get some money." She reached into her pocket and felt her credit card. "My credit card won't work here in 1922," she whispered. Glancing at her watch, she decided there was time to get back to 2018 and then return to1922 to buy clothes by the time she had to meet Jack.

She looked into the mirror over the dresser. *I look like a mess.* She picked up her purse and pulled her makeup kit from it and ran into the bathroom. Splashing some water on her face, she patted it dry with a small, rose hand towel and refreshed her makeup.

Running back to the elevator, after she locked the door to her room, she waited. It seemed to be stuck on the first floor. *It's taking too long.* She stuffed the key in her pocket, ran down the staircase to the lobby, and pushed through the revolving front door.

She stopped on the top step of the hotel entrance stairs. She raised her hand to shade her eyes and looked around the driveway to make sure Jack was nowhere in sight. She stood for a minute and got her bearings. *Let's see. The gazebo is that way.*

Stepping onto the pavement, she looked back at the hotel. A flutter of the curtain in her room caught her eye. She glanced up. A shadow moved. The tip of a cigarette glowed. *It might be the ghost. I don't have time to go back.* She turned left, went straight ahead, and then ran in the direction of the murder scene.

When she reached the gazebo, she looked around. Everything was quiet. The press and crowd that lurked at Walsh's home were gone. Yellow tape still covered the front door of 4B. Walsh's nameplate was still attached to the front of the bungalow. "Things are not quite back to normal." She ran up the steps of the gazebo, two at a time. Flopping down on the bench, she waited. "I hope this works. Dark clouds, biding their time, drifted toward the gazebo. A mist began to form. It swirled around the gazebo enclosing it.

Hollywood, 2018

The mist cleared. Daisy glanced around. The grass and flowers vanished. Stores and restaurants sat on a blacktop parking lot. Daisy sat on the gazebo bench in front of and across the street from the apothecary. She wiped droplets of the mist from her face with the back of her hand. "No time to waste," she whispered. Jumping off the bench, she raced to the street. Her limo was gone. *I wonder what happened to John. Poor man. By now, he must have reported me missing. The police may be looking for me.* Glancing to her left, she saw the Bank of America building. On the light pole next to the building, she saw a picture of herself. Over the image, her name was listed. Under the picture, her name and a phone number to call if seen. She searched her purse and found her sunglasses. Grabbing them, she slipped them on and pushed them to the bridge of her nose. *Hopefully, these will keep me from being recognized.*

She pushed up the sleeve of her shirt and glanced at her watch. *I have ten minutes until the bank closes. Thank goodness I have my credit card.* She reached deep into her pocket and removed the card. "How much will I need?" She thought for a minute. "More than the ATM will spit out, I'm sure. They're getting ready to close, but I still have time to slip in and get to a teller. They haven't locked the door yet." She pulled open the heavy glass door next to her. The lines were long. She glanced around the room and rushed to the teller with the least people. She hoped the woman didn't know anything about her disappearance.

When it was her turn, the teller looked at Daisy over the rims of her glasses. She smiled. "I saw you come in. You just made it." She pushed her glasses to the bridge of her nose and lifted herself over her counter so that she could look at Daisy's jeans. "And what happened to you?"

"Hi, Sandy." She looked at the teller's name tag and glanced down at her clothes. The bloodstain was now dark brown. "I had some mud splashed on me from a huge puddle by a passing motorist while I was crossing the road near the back of the parking lot. I know I look a mess, but I didn't have time to change and get here before the bank closed."

"It almost looks like blood."

"Heavens, no! Just mud."

"I'll make sure I watch out for the puddle," the teller said.

Sandy smiled. "You look very much like someone on a poster I've seen."

"Nope, not me. They say everyone has a double. Must be something like that."

"What can I do for you?"

Daisy smiled back "I'm going on a trip. At the last minute, I realized I need more cash than I have now." She slid her card into the reader and punched in her code. "I need fifteen hundred dollars, please."

"Do you think you'll have enough?" the teller asked. Her expression grew serious.

"Yes. It should be."

The bank clerk reached into the drawer beside her and pulled out several stacks of banded bills. After counting out fifteen hundred dollars, she smiled. "May I put the bills in a plain envelope for you?"

"Yes. Thank you for your help. I'll use my card if I need more." She didn't add, "After I leave 1922 and get back here to 2018."

Daisy glanced at her watch. *My trips back and forth don't seem to take too long. I'll have enough time to shop for1922 clothes before Jack gets to the hotel for our dinner date. That is if the mist at the gazebo cooperates.*

Hollywood CA 1922

Daisy, walking to the gazebo, thought about stopping at her favorite Mexican restaurant for a snack. *No time.* She looked up. Dark clouds swelled in the sky. Feeling drops of rain, she ran. When she reached the apothecary, she turned, crossed the street, and raced to the gazebo. Before she could sit on the bench, the weather changed again. She felt the warmth from the sun. Looking across the road, she saw the house at 4B and shivered.

She turned and walked on the path leading away from the spot where the murder occurred, past the emerald fields. *Let's see, the man at the hotel's registration desk said I would be able to find some boutiques between the larger stores.* Soon the street turned to a more commercial neighborhood. She hunted for a clothing store. Looking up and down the main road, she decided to explore some of the side streets for a women's clothing store. She looked at the women that passed by her. *They have really gotten rid of the shackles of the Victorian era. Their hips are emphasized. Well, my hips aren't bad. I should be okay. They're more informal. Not as casual as today, but casual.*

She peeked down a side street in the middle of the second block and stopped. A sign attached to a pole pointed to a boutique down an alley on her right. She walked toward it. The small shop at the end of the narrow passageway was squeezed between a department store and a hardware store. She laughed, peeking into its front window. "It looks like a costume shop."

Pushing the door open, she stood for a few minutes and looked around a large open room filled with all sorts of women's clothes. They hung on hangers on racks and stands. *I need some clothes, so I fit in and not look like a character in a western movie. Though no one seems to stare at me. They probably think I'm in the cast of a movie. Only the bank teller noticed the dried blood and who I might be. At least I escaped before she figured out it was me on the flyer.*

"May I help you?"

She looked in the direction of the voice and smiled at the woman behind a counter at the back of the large room. She wore a very stylish dress that hid her well-built frame. Her brown hair was short in a fashionable bob with bangs.

"I need a few outfits. There was a problem where I live, and I have to start over."

"You poor dear. What are you looking for?"

"Some things that are casual for day and some flashy dresses for evening. I also need shoes and undergarments.

"Casual clothes are on the racks in this room. Dressing rooms and dressy outfits are in a room behind me, along with lingerie. When you're ready, I'll take you back there." She pointed behind her.

"Thank you." Daisy looked at the racks of clothes. She wandered among them and stopped at the size four section. After she looked at the price tags, she began to select some informal clothes. She smiled. *I'm using 2018 money. I can get a lot of things.* She pulled a navy sweater from a rack. Looking down, she held it against herself and moved to a narrow mirror on the wall where she could make a better assessment. The sweater had pockets and hung below her hips. *Perfect.* She threw it over her arm, then looked for more clothes. Next, she picked a gray skirt with stitched down pleats and two pairs of slacks, one brown, one navy, and a brown wool jacket. She placed everything on the glass counter. Pulling two white blouses from the rack, she added them to her selections. She stared at the clerk. "I need a few dresses."

"Are you one of the actors from the Western they're making near here?"

"Something like that."

"I thought so. But, I've never seen you in a movie."

"I'm new in Hollywood. This will be my first job." She smiled. "I also need a couple of casual dresses."

"They're on the rack against the wall on the other side of the room."

"Thanks." Daisy quickly walked to the rack. She chose an emerald green with canary yellow and bright red flowers, and a navy blue with a sailor collar. *No, I don't want navy.* She hung it back on the bar. *Think I'll take the royal purple.* She pulled both from their hangers. Walking back to the mirror, she studied them as she held them in front of her. The dresses had low waists and square necklines. She felt their soft cotton material between her fingers. She added them to the other clothes on the counter. "Can I look at the dressy selections now?"

"Don't you want to try on anything?"

Daisy glanced at her watch. "I know they will be fine."

The clerk pulled open the low wooden door. "Follow me." She led Daisy to a doorway behind the counter and into the room in front of her. It was filled with beaded, sequined, and fringed dresses. Thumbing through the dresses hanging in her size, she thought for a second. "Let's see. I'll take the black and the peacock blue." She looked at the clerk as she took the dresses from their hanger, turned, and walked toward the front room. "Wait, I think I'll try one of them on."

"Just go there." The clerk pointed across the room.

Daisy moved behind the screen and slipped out of her clothes. She held both dresses in front of her and glanced in the mirror on the wall. Pulling the black dress over her head, she pulled up the back zipper, walked out into the room, and looked into the full-length mirror to get a better view. She studied herself. "I love it." She shook herself and watched the beads shine and the fringe bounce. "Of course, it would look better without the boots," she said to the clerk.

The woman laughed. "The colors you selected go well with your auburn hair. They are both excellent choices for you."

"You can add them to the other clothes." Daisy handed both dresses to the lady. "Oh, I also need some shoes. How about a pair of T-strap, low-heeled, brown leather and another pair in the same style in black, silk." She dressed in her clothes as she talked.

"What size?"

"Seven. Seven, narrow."

The clerk pulled two boxes from slots in the wall behind her and laid them on the counter.

"I'll try them. Shoes can be difficult." She sat in the chair near the counter and eased out of the boots. Taking the brown shoes from the box, she slipped them on. She stood and took s few steps. "They are just right." *I'm not crazy about the shoes. I prefer the high thin heels of our time. But, they go with the times. So I'll learn to like them.* She sighed.

"Anything else?" the clerk pointed to the area of accessories in the glass case on top of the counter.

"Let's see. Several undergarments. Pink, white, and beige."

"Any accessories?"

Daisy studied the accessories. "Add that long strand of pearls, the blue and black scarf and the yellow scarf with the fringe. Earrings. I think I'll take the long, dangling gold ones. The only thing left is that brown, close-fitting felt hat with the flowers and a headband with the feathers." *I never thought of accessories.*

Daisy flipped through the price tags and mentally added her purchases as the clerk added her last requests. *I'll have lots of money left over. More than enough to pay the hotel bill.*

Daisy smiled hearing the clang of the cash register each time an outfit was added to the bill. *Bet this has been her biggest sale all week.*

The clerk handed her the bill and waited. "Can I offer you a cup of tea?"

"No, thank you. As you can see, I'm in a bit of a hurry."

I was just about right. Daisy dug into the pocket of her jeans and removed the envelope. She pulled out the amount she needed for her purchase and handed the money to the woman. *I wish I could get this many outfits for this amount today.*

She pulled on her boots as she waited for her clothes to be neatly folded in tissue paper and slipped into shopping bags.

"Where can I buy some makeup?"

"Right after the department store, there's a small shop at the end of the alley. You'll be able to get what you need."

"Thanks."

"Please come again," the clerk said, watching Daisy gather the bags and hurry to the front door of the boutique.

"Thank you for all your help. I would stay and chat, but as I said, I'm late. Next time. I'll be back." Daisy threw the words over her shoulder as she pushed through the door and ran to the cosmetics store. She threw open the door and studied the clerk behind the counter for a few minutes. *Her makeup looks like I should look if I'm going to fit into the 1920s.* She quickly picked out some dark mascara, green eyeshadow, dark-brown liner and brows, and very red lipstick.

The clerk wrapped the makeup in tissue paper. "The green eyeshadow will look good on you."

"Thanks," Daisy said. "I don't need a bag. I'll just tuck it in one of my shopping bags."

She squinted at her watch. *I just have time to get back to the hotel, change my clothes, and read over the report Jack left with me.* She ran down the street, took the hotel stairs two at a time, and pushed through the front door. She hurried to the front desk. "Key, please." She smiled at the front desk clerk. "Did I get any messages?"

He turned and looked into cubby-hole 313. "No, Miss O'Malley. The key doesn't seem to be here."

"Who would have taken it?" She looked around the lobby and thought for a moment. She pushed her hand in her pocket "Sorry, I forgot to leave it. I kept it with me."

Who would call me? No one knows me in this lifetime except for Jack and some of the players in the murder. I don't think any of them would call me.

She rushed to the elevators and pushed the "up" button. Her shopping bags rustled against each other. Waiting, she stared at the arrow above the door of the elevator. It moved slowly from the fifth floor to the lobby. She heard it bounce, and the gate slid back. No one was there. She stared. The ghosts didn't show themselves. She felt someone standing next to her and turned, hoping it was the ghost trying to make contact again. She jumped.

"Jack, it's you." She watched him walk through an arched doorway from the gardens. "I'm so sorry. I'm late, and I'm not ready. I didn't have time to read the report you left with me."

He smiled. "Calm down. Don't worry. We'll look it over at dinner. I was afraid you went out and got lost."

"No, I needed a few things."

"It looks as if you bought out a store." He looked at her shopping bags. A chuckle echoed in his voice.

"It's just a few things. It won't take me long to change."

"All right, I'll be right here. I'll read the newspaper and see what they have to say about the murder today. Each day the news floats a different idea on who the murderer is." He waved as he walked toward a couch in the lobby and sat.

She flew into the elevator. *Darn. The operator isn't here again.* She turned the crank. It didn't move. "Oh, my goodness, I have to close the gate, then turn the crank. *Calm down, Daisy, calm down. Jack's not upset.* She thought about the steps she had seen the operator perform to make the elevator work. Now she was doing it correctly. The elevator moved; she didn't feel alone. She could smell the scent of gardenia perfume.

When the elevator landed on her floor, she heard footsteps. A cool breeze covered her. A voice whispered, "Good evening." The ghosts of the man and woman showed themselves.

"We waited in your room. You were gone for a long time. We had to get to the dancehall in Venice Beach for a dance contest and finally had to leave," the man said.

"Oh, I'm sorry I don't have time talk to you now."

"We'll talk later." The woman smiled.

Desmond and a blonde woman danced by her in the direction of the end of the hallway.

Even in death, he connects with blondes. She laughed.

"Wait," she yelled. "Tell me who murdered you. That should only take a minute." She heard a loud sigh, and the ghosts disappeared. *It was the ghosts in my room when I left for shopping.* She felt bad about being in a hurry and not being able to talk with them.

CHAPTER SIX

Daisy ran to the bathroom and turned on the cold and hot faucets of the bathtub. She flipped on the shower knob, wanting the water just warm enough for her to hop in. While the water warmed, she unpacked and meticulously hung some of the new clothes. After folding the other clothes, she placed them in the dresser drawers. Lastly, she tucked her 2018 cosmetic kit in the upper drawer of the dresser. Leaving her sweater, brown slacks, blouse and matching undergarments on the bed, she grabbed her new makeup and set it on top of the shelf below the bathroom sink's mirror.

She dropped her clothes on the bathroom floor, ran her hand under the shower water, and climbed over the side of the tub. The water ran over her. She relaxed for minute and rubbed a bar of soap over herself, then quickly rinsed off. Grabbing a large royal blue towel on the rack beside the tub, she climbed out of the bathtub and wrapped it around herself. She jumped from foot to foot. *Boy, this tile floor is cold.* Patting her face dry, she carefully applied new makeup.

She glanced in the mirror over the dresser, where she could see the full effect and smiled. *I like the twenties look.* Careful not to disturb her makeup, she pulled on the clothes she left on the bed and pulled her hair in a tight bun, letting wisps of curls hang around her face. *Now I look more like a twenty's person.* Taking a minute, to decide between a scarf and dangling earrings, she let both win. She draped the yellow scarf around her shoulders. *Finally, I'm ready.*

"Where's my key? Where did I put it?" She glanced around the room. "Let's see. I came into the room, put my new clothes away, and went into the bathroom..." She looked in the dresser drawers. "Here it is. I dropped it beside my old makeup kit." Daisy grabbed her key and ran to the door.

"Wait, there's something else. What am I missing?" She rested her hand on her hip and looked around the room. She ran into the bathroom, grabbed her clothes on the floor, and threw open the closet. Taking one of her shopping bags, she stuffed her jeans and sweater into it. Opening the room door, she dropped it on the floor. "They'll be cleaned and ready for me to dress in when I leave 1922." *There's something else.* She stood at the open door and looked around the room. "The folder." Hurrying to the bed, she reached for it and tucked it under her arm. She pulled the door closed, slipped her key in the lock, turned it, and waited for the click. She twisted the doorknob to make sure it was secure.

Deciding between the elevator and stairs, she opted for the elevator when she saw it sitting with an opened gate. *Where is the operator, and why did he come to the third floor and leave it with the gate opened? Where is he?*

Daisy felt herself trip as she entered the elevator.

"Be careful."

She hadn't heard the operator approach her and jumped with surprise at the voice as she turned. The operator stood very close behind her, causing her to bump into him.

"Sorry, I didn't quite land even with the third floor. I thought I would have time to take a break and get back before anyone needed a ride."

"Don't worry. It's okay. No harm done. She watched him close the gate. He turned the controls to the left. The elevator crept downward. She stood in the back and went over the events of the murder and the women in Desmond Walsh's life. *One of them might not be a friend, but an enemy.*

When she reached the lobby, she watched the operator push the "stop" button. He nodded to her and pulled back the gate.

"Thanks." Her eyes searched the room for Jack. He stood at the registration desk and was the only person in the room. *Thank goodness. No casual conversation with the clerk, perhaps getting a hint about when and how I arrived.*

He looked up when he heard her footsteps clicking on the marble floor. "That was quick." He tossed the newspaper onto the chair next to the desk.

"I almost forgot the info you gave me to read. I didn't have time to go over it." She handed the file to him when she reached him.

"Don't worry about it. Like I said before, we'll go over the folder at dinner." He looked at her and smiled. "It's a beautiful evening. We're going to the Armstrong and Carlton Café. It's just a couple of blocks away. Is a walk all right with you?"

"That will be nice. I love to walk." Daisy walked beside him. She slowed to a stop when she heard the sound of jazz, mellow and sad, flow from a wall where a large man stood. "What kind of club is that, and where is the door?"

"It's a speakeasy. The door is well hidden. You'll see. I made reservations for tomorrow night. The speakeasies are run mainly by criminals of the underworld, or as they're called, the Mafia. Prohibition has not only brought the illegal sale of bootleg alcohol, but gambling, and crime."

"I've read hordes of people come to California for the sunshine, warm weather, and fortune."

"That's right. However, many have only found poverty. Some death. This happened when these people became involved with the fringe element. They are the people who can't seem to find success and lived on the edge, getting involved in drugs and crime to make their lives seem not so bad."

"What about the police? Don't they do anything?"

"Most of them look the other way and let the criminals operate undisturbed. Some of them take bribes. My captain seems honest. Haven't discovered anything crooked about him, yet."

"What did the paper say about the murder?"

"They just rehashed what is already known. There's no new news. The case will probably be in the headlines until it is solved. Hollywood people make news all over the country. Everyone is interested in their lives, especially if it's a troubled one."

Daisy glimpsed at the sign, A and C Café, in blue and red letters. "We're here."

"Hope you brought your appetite." He took her arm and guided her to the front door of the restaurant.

"I'm famished. The only thing I've had all day is a couple of cups of coffee and a sweet roll." She climbed the four steps to the cafe door.

She followed him through the door and watched him nod to the man standing behind the podium. "Two please, Samuel. Somewhere quiet."

"Yes, Detective Donovan. I have a table for two in the back."

"Thanks." Jack put his hand on her waist and guided her to another short flight of stairs to a table in a dimly lit alcove. "What would you like to drink?" Jack asked.

"Can I get some white wine?"

"Yes." He turned to Samuel. "This restaurant smuggles in wine from Europe."

"A white wine for the lady and a double scotch on the rocks for me, please," Jack said.

"We just got a shipment from France, Detective Donovan."

Her eyebrows raised in amazement. "It seems people find ways to get around the Eighteenth Amendment."

Jack smiled. "You can bring the drinks. Give us a few minutes."

"Yes, sir."

"Do you come here often?" She wondered if he had a significant other. Someone he sat in the dim light with and spoke to softly.

"Not often. Sometimes, I come with other detectives to celebrate the successful ending of a case."

She looked down at the table. A warning voice whispered in her head. *Don't get too close. Help with this case and go back to 2018.* Her hands in her lap were hidden from sight. They twisted nervously. Feeling his stare, she lifted her head. Their eyes met. *I can't get involved. This is 1922, and I'm from 2018.* She gave an anxious little cough.

"Shall we get to the report?" Jack opened the manila folder. He pushed it toward her so they could both read.

"Before we start, why are we going to a speakeasy? Don't get me wrong. I'm looking forward to it. How does it help the case?"

"Well, what the Chief didn't mention when we were at the station, was what others are saying. Walsh was working with federal prosecutors before his death, to help find out who supplied the drugs. He wanted them to get them arrested and sent to jail. Hollywood is becoming overrun with drugs, and the drugs are bringing crime. Some in the department believe Walsh got too close to the identity of the dealers supplying Hollywood. I believe that's why he was killed."

When the waiter returned with the drinks, he set the wine in front of her. Daisy waited for him to leave, raised her glass, and took a sip of wine. "Let's look at the list of Walsh's friends and work associates. Maybe the two of us can figure out the person who might have enough against him to commit murder." Daisy scanned the file Jack flipped open and pushed near her, so they could both look at it.

"It is never that easy. I think we can eliminate Pryor. I believe he has disappeared in the woods of Canada. There have been no reports of him trying to cross from the Canadian border back into the United States. However, we still have the border patrol looking out for him, just in case." Jack pulled his pen from his breast pocket and drew a line through Pryor's name, crossing him out. "What about Peavey?"

"Remember, I was there when he entered the house. I think his reaction to the death of his employer was genuine. He seemed very surprised when he saw Walsh's body. He looked almost afraid. Also, he doesn't seem to have a motive for the crime and has been cooperative."

"Okay, he's off the list too." He put his pen back after he slid a black line, crossing Peavey's name off the list." Jack motioned to the waiter.

"Are you ready to order?" the waiter asked when he reached their table.

"Yes."

Daisy quickly scanned the menu. "I think I'll have a mixed salad, salmon, and assorted vegetables."

"Sounds good. Make that two." Jack smiled. "And bring a bottle of the wine the lady is drinking and another wine glass."

Jack pushed the folder to the side of the table, making space for the meals when they arrived. Folding back the cover, he scanned the list. "There are three women with M for the first initials of their first names. Remember the letters signed M?"

"Well, let's see Mabel Vidor. We talked to her at the station. I've read in the tabloids Walsh was deeply in love with her. She was the last person to see him alive, except for the murderer."

"Mabel's driver gave Peavey and her alibis when he confirmed he gave Peavey a ride to his house and then took her home. When he left Walsh's and drove them home, he said Walsh was alive. We can cross her off the list." He reached back into the inside breast pocket of his jacket and pulled out the pen. Removing the cap, he drew a line through Mabel's name.

"Charles Miller gave us some information on Walsh's friends."

"I think what he said didn't mean much. He was just trying to get out from under our radar." Daisy replied.

"If Charles Miller works with the federal people and is connected to the Mafia, he might have been reporting to the Mafia what Walsh discovered and what went on at the District Attorney meetings. He might have been the one who knows who committed the murder of Desmond Walsh or who ordered it."

"I believe the real question is about his loyalty to the Mafia. I don't believe the reason he gave for trying to get upstairs the day Walsh was found."

"I agree that he wasn't telling the truth. We need another interview with him."

"I concur." Daisy smiled. "He probably was looking for a hiding place in a wall or drawer."

"We looked carefully. There was no such place."

"Next, we have Mary Miles Giroux," Daisy said.

"She is as old as the daughter he abandoned. If those were her letters, she was having more than a friendship with him."

"By the letters I read, I'm not sure she's living in the real world. Well, there are two women that thought he was going to marry them."

Jack laughed. "Mary has a younger sister. The sisters seem to have a strange relationship."

"What about the former wife and daughter?" Daisy asked.

"I've put them last on the list. Apparently, they thought Walsh was dead until they saw him in a Picture Palace one night. I don't think they're here now. Apparently, they came to Hollywood at the request of Walsh's lawyer. Walsh wanted to set up his Will so his daughter inherited his money and belongings, with the mother's supervision. I think they went back to New York after they met with Walsh and his lawyer. I tried to contact the mother. They are not at the hotel where they stayed when they arrived."

"Where were they staying?"

"At the same hotel where you're staying."

"I haven't seen them in the lobby."

"Here's our dinner."

Daisy took a sip of wine. "It looks good." She stabbed her fork into the salmon and took a bite. "It is." She took another piece and laid her fork down. "Who's next on the list?"

"Well, let's see." He tasted his fish. "You're right. The fish is good."

"Charlotte Miles. She's Mary Giroux's mother. The tabloids don't have anything nice to say about her. The rumor is she manipulates the people around her daughter to further the girl's career. She also has some kind of bitter financial dispute with her daughter. There's a lawsuit brewing—daughter against mother. The mother takes care of the disabled child, Beth. She makes sure no one sees the girl so she can't be interviewed. The mother is afraid she might say something to ruin her sister."

"It's a well-known fact, the mother is on a first-name basis with the Los Angeles District Attorney and has been his date for many social events. We would have difficulty getting any info from her that she doesn't want to share. If she complains to the District Attorney that we are putting pressure on her, he would come to her defense and stop our questions." Jack sighed.

He looked at Daisy. "Why don't you eat before your dinner gets cold? I'll read the last two suspects." He took a big bite of his salmon.

"Charlotte Miles also had some big problem with Walsh. No one knows what it was about."

Daisy picked up her fork and began to eat.

"There is Margaret Palmer. Another actress who worked with Walsh and Charles Miller. Her picture was on the wall at the house. You don't hear much about her."

"We have quite a list to interview, and three of the women are blondes. It will be interesting to find out whose hair was on his jacket."

"It was probably Mabel Vidor's hair. She said she hugged him before she left," Daisy said.

"All of the women on the list are in the photographs on Walsh's walls. Since I have a small part in a movie with Margaret Palmer, I'll make friends with her and see what I can find out. Maybe she knows something about the murder. She's working as an extra. I think it's strange; she's been in Hollywood for a long time. Maybe she'll be willing to share something about Walsh with me." Daisy told another white lie, but she was sure she could go on the set of the movie Margaret Palmer was in and mingle with the crowd of extras.

"Tomorrow, we start watching them at the funeral. It's always interesting to see who makes an appearance at the cemetery and their reaction. Are you free to go to the funeral?"

"You bet. They're not shooting the scenes I'm in." *A little white lie again is okay. I just have to figure out how I can sneak on the set as an extra. Then it won't be a lie.*

"The funeral is at eleven. I'll pick you up at ten-thirty.

"I'll be ready."

He looked at her empty plate. "I guess we're finished unless you want dessert."

"No, thanks. I've had enough, and the wine made me very sleepy. I need to get to my room at the hotel."

He motioned to the waiter. "Tab, please." After the waiter handed him the check, Jack glanced at it. He drew some bills from his pocket and pressed the bill and money into the waiter's hand.

"Thank you very much, Detective Donovan." The server smiled.

"Yes, thank you. The dinner was delicious," Daisy said as she stood.

"Can you make the walk to the hotel?"

"Sure. The exercise will do me good. I need to walk off my dinner."

"What's going on?" Daisy stopped at the door. She heard sirens and watched a group of police cars screech to a stop near them. Police jumped out of the cars and ran toward the restaurant.

Jack pulled her to the side of the doorway. "They're raiding the restaurant. They think there's a speakeasy entrance somewhere around here. They'll never find it."

She hurried, following him to the side of the building. "Why do they bother?"

"Well, they have to show the temperance ladies they're trying to stop the flow of bootleg whiskey. It's all for show." He laughed. "They'll pretend to search."

Daisy watched the patrons being led from the restaurant and told to leave. "I don't see any alcohol."

"They ditched their drinks when they heard the sirens."

"I guess they didn't find any alcohol and certainly didn't find a speakeasy. I don't see the bartender being led away."

He grabbed her hand and led her out of the path of the police. He didn't let go as they walked.

The weather had changed since they entered the restaurant. The moon hid behind thick, black clouds. It was a starless night. A gentle sprinkling started.

"We better run." Jack pulled her along behind him.

"Rain comes at the worst time."

When they reached the hotel, he ducked into the lobby and walked her to the elevator. "Are you all right?" He watched her breathing heavily.

"I'm fine. Just a little winded." She pushed the button on the wall next to the elevator and watched the arrow above the elevator slide down from the third floor. *I wonder if the ghosts will revisit me.*

Jack leaned close and gave her a kiss on the top of her head, turned, and walked to the front door of the hotel. "See you tomorrow." He threw the words over his shoulder.

She waved as the elevator bounced to a stop. When the operator pulled back the gate, she stepped in.

He smiled at her. "Nice evening."

"Yes. Until the rain started." She walked to the back of the elevator and looked around. *No ghosts. I hope they will be in the hallway near my room.*

When the elevator stopped, she looked around. No luck.

CHAPTER SEVEN

Daisy lay wide-awake tossing and turning. She didn't remember drifting off to sleep until a loud knock on the door made her sit straight up. "Just a minute. I'm coming," she called out. *Who can that be?* She laid back down, tempted to ignore the knock and snuggle under the covers until she saw the morning light peek through a small opening of the curtains. The sun bounced off the mirror, sending sparkling light around the room. *Who is at my door? I didn't leave a wakeup call.*

She tossed back the duvet, slid out of bed, and threw the chenille throw at the end of the bed around her shoulders. She heard the knock again. "I'll be right there." Running across the floor with bare feet and bleary eyes, she reached the door and pulled it open. Sun shining through the window at the end of the hall to her right lit the corridor. No one stood outside her door. She looked to her left and saw a man at the end of the hall. "Wait. Please wait. What do you want?"

She saw the blood on his jacket as he turned and stared at her.

"Keep looking," he whispered and walked into the wall. "Make sure they get punished."

"I must be losing it," she murmured. "I either need a hot shower or more sleep."

She glanced at her watch; a hot shower won. She ran into the bathroom and turned the faucet with an H etched into it.

Somehow, I need to get the ghost to stay around longer. He must know who murdered him. If he doesn't, he might be able to give me a clue. This morning I'm going to relax and soak in the bathtub. She went to the closet and picked out some clothes. Returning to the bath, she looked around. The water was so hot the mirror over the sink fogged. She grabbed a towel and wiped away the mist. Immediately, she shut off the hot water and turned on the cold water. In a few seconds, she touched the water with her fingertips. "That's better."

Climbing over the side of the tub, she slid down until she submerged to her chin. Closing her eyes, she relaxed and thought about her trip into 1922. *This is becoming an exciting trip. Why did I slip back into 1922? Why was I selected to help with the investigation? Who cares, I'm part of it now, and I'm going to stay until we find the murderer.*

After a short while with no conclusion about what was happening and why, she climbed from the tub, wrapping a fluffy towel around herself. *The plan is for me to meet Jack later this morning for the funeral. I think I'll dress and go by the movie set near here. It will be a quick trip. Maybe one of the women on the list will be there, or perhaps someone will talk about Walsh's murder. Hopefully, Margaret Palmer will be there.*

She dressed quickly in her gray skirt, white blouse, and navy sweater. She stood in front of the mirror, brushed her hair, and applied her makeup. "I like the twenties look. I wish it would come back." Slipping on her shoes, she pushed her new brown hat on her head and stuck a handkerchief in her pocket, grabbed the room key, and threw open the door, hoping the ghost would be there again. She wasn't that lucky.

"What's hanging on the doorknob? Oh, my jeans and shirt are back." She tossed them in the closet next to her boots. *They're clean and ready for my trip back to 2018.* Running back to the door, she let it slam shut behind her, locked it, and ran down the stairs. Pushing through the front door, she dashed down the street to the movie set near the hotel.

When she reached the set, she sat on a bench with a group of actors and actresses holding their scripts and running lines with each other while they waited to be called for their scene. "It's a Western. I should have on the clothes I was wearing when I traveled into the 1920s," she whispered.

"Did you say something to me?" the woman next to Daisy asked, leaning closer to her.

"Oh no, I was just talking to myself."

She began to make small talk with the woman. "I assume the actors and actresses with large parts are somewhere else. Are you working as an extra, or do you have a small part?" Daisy asked.

"Trying to break into films. I have a very small part. I get to say two lines. How about you?"

Hearing someone sobbing, Daisy stopped and turned. *It was coming from the end of the aisle.*

"Excuse me, I'll be right back," she said, sliding down an empty row of seats and sat next to a young woman with short, curly blonde hair and soulful brown eyes. Tears welled in her eyes and found their way down her cheeks.

"What's wrong?" Daisy asked.

"I was so in love with him. I can't believe he's been murdered." Her voice was very low.

"Who are you talking about?" Daisy leaned close to her.

"Desmond. We had a long relationship. He was the love of my life."

"How long did you know him?"

"We met in Arizona in a little theater. We were in several plays together. We had a lovely affair. Then, one day he was gone." She wiped her eyes. "He told me he was restless and decided to travel through Canada. He said he might see me again. When I saw him again in Hollywood, he told me he served in the Canadian army before he got into films here. He said he was sorry he left me. I forgave him right away, and we began to see each other again."

Daisy smiled and took the handkerchief from her pocket. She wiped a smudge of makeup from the girl's cheek and dabbed her eyes. "What's your name?"

"I'm Margaret Gibson Palmer."

Another woman on the list with an initial M. "Did you work with him when you came to Hollywood?"

"We were in four movies together. In two of them, I had substantial parts."

"Did you start a relationship with him again?"

"For a while. I was doing quite well and had a very nice bungalow in Santa Monica. It overlooked the Pacific Ocean. Unfortunately, I got in with some bad characters I met at the speakeasy near Walsh's house. I got arrested under the Mann Act. The charges were dropped, but Desmond wouldn't have anything to do with me. I tried and tried, but I couldn't make him change his mind. He never forgave me."

Daisy thought for a minute. *The Mann Act. Let's see.* Her brow furrowed. *If I remember my history, the Mann Act had to do with prostitution.*

"The word got around. Now, I just get minor roles." She sniffed, stopped, and listened. "They're calling my scene. I have to go."

"So do I." Daisy glanced at her watch. "I guess I'll see you at the funeral?"

"Yes, you will."

Daisy took her hand. "You'll be okay. Things will get better."

Funeral

"Where is Walsh being buried?" Daisy asked. Grabbing the door handle, she slid into the front seat of the police car.

"At Oakley Memorial Park. It's on the north-slope at the east end of the Santa Monica Mountain range. It overlooks Hollywood. It's a beautiful place, filled with towering evergreen trees, weeping willows dipping into the lakes, sweeping lawns, splashing fountains, rolling hills, and beautiful statuary. Dirt paths twist and turn through the gravesites. There are benches along the paths so people can sit on warm sunny days and read or contemplate. Before it was a cemetery, it was a filming area for many epic movies."

"There's a service in a chapel first, then the burial."

"Who arranged the funeral?"

"I assume his lawyer."

Daisy stared as Jack veered off the main road, slowed down, and parked his patrol car under a weeping willow, next to a bubbling stream. His car was last in a line of limos.

Daisy glanced out the window. She got out of the car and stood under the weeping willow tree. Its branches bent over like an umbrella. "It looks like a park. It's so beautiful." She heard birds chirping.

"We're the last ones here," Jack whispered. He took her arm, and they slipped into the chapel, sitting in the last row.

Daisy looked at the stained-glass windows and followed the service in the prayer book. Embroidered flowers embellished the kneeling pads. She waited for the service to conclude and the pallbearers carry the casket to the gravesite next to the chapel.

"This will be close enough." Jack stopped her a few feet from the chapel. "We have a good view of everyone." He pointed to the group of people next to a small lake and a rectangular stone with an angel on top.

"The women sitting in the front row listened to the service. They look so glamorous dressed in black dresses, even with black veils over their faces. I didn't get a good look at them in the chapel, but each also has perfectly coiffed hair. Look at them. They dab their eyes, making sure their makeup isn't smudged."

"They're movie stars and know the paparazzi will be at the funeral photographing them. Some of the people are tourists and are taking photos to show their relatives back home. Look at the press tripping over each other and pushing each other out of the way so they can get the best pictures for their newspapers."

"What about the people on the hill, behind the gravesite, near the mourners?" Daisy pointed to her left and a small group of men and women.

"Just more people wanting to see who is at the funeral. They got here early enough to get good seats and a view."

"Do you think any of them will ask for autographs?"

"No. they're usually pretty good. Plus, I'm sure they've seen my patrol car and will behave."

"Peavey is the only one that looks genuinely upset. The women are posing for the cameras of the press standing near them. They are patting their eyes. It looks to me as if they are pretending to cry," Daisy said.

"Who is the man standing with his hat hiding his face, next to a couple of repulsive-looking men?"

"They are Mafia, and that's Charles Miller standing with them. Even though he denies it, he's with them often. You'll meet him again and the men he's with when we go to the speakeasy."

"I didn't recognize Miller with his hat pulled down, hiding his face. He says he is an agent in Hollywood and supposedly a friend of Walsh. At least the newspaper quoted him as saying he was deeply disturbed by his dear friend's death."

"If he hangs with criminals, do you think he kept the actors and actresses appraised of the movement of drugs and where to get them?"

"We'll find out."

"Who are the woman and young girl standing away from the group?" Daisy pointed again. "They don't look like Hollywood types."

"I don't know who they are. Maybe the woman is the former wife and the young woman his daughter."

"They sat alone in the last row on the other side of the chapel across from us. I don't think strangers would have come to the service in the chapel," Daisy whispered.

"Could be. Perhaps the wife and daughter didn't leave after all."

"They're not very dressed up. Just in everyday clothes, not anything like Hollywood people."

"Let's talk with them after the service is over."

After the priest said the final prayer, the group began to leave. Each one got into a limo alone.

Jack took Daisy's hand and pulled her with him. He tried to catch up with the woman and her daughter.

"Mrs. Walsh. It is Mrs. Walsh, isn't it?" he asked when he got close to her at the limo.

The woman turned. "Yes. Well, it was. It's Mrs. Donaldson now."

"I'm Detective Donovan, and this is Miss O'Malley. We'd like to talk with you. Where are you staying?"

"I'm at my former husband's house. The Lieutenant Governor made an exception for us and let us stay there. He was nice and provided us with a limo and driver. He had the house cleaned for us. You can stop by later this afternoon. Say about two?"

"Thank you. We'll be there."

Jack guided Daisy to the patrol car. As the limos pulled away from Oakley Memorial Park, they stood surveying the cemetery. "Let's go see Mary Miles Giroux. She should be home by the time we get to her house."

"I believe I saw her in the crowd at Walsh's house the morning of the murder, and I also saw a photo of her on the wall at Walsh's house," Daisy said.

"That was quite a group at the funeral," Daisy commented after she got back in the car. "The women looked as if they were acting."

"Actresses never stop acting."

She turned toward him, ignoring his last statement. "I forgot to tell you. Before you picked me up, I went for a walk to the set near the hotel to snoop around. I met Margaret Gibson Palmer, another woman who was very much in love with Walsh. The affair started when she met him in Arizona and started up again in Hollywood. However, he didn't return the love. She thought they might get together again, but when she faced prostitution charges, he wouldn't bother with her. She tried to convince him she would straighten out and that the allegations were a misunderstanding and would never happen again. It did no good. After the arrest, her life turned bad. She lives in a small apartment near Walsh's bungalow. After talking to her, I don't think she murdered him. She's just sorry she lost him."

Visit to Mary Miles Giroux

"We're here." Jack smiled.

"That was fast."

Daisy watched the scenery when Jack drove up a long driveway, lined with small hedges on either side. The Spanish-style house wasn't a cottage or a mansion, but a medium-sized home in a quiet neighborhood. She loved the white stucco walls and terra cotta tile roof. A fountain with bubbling water sat in the middle of a circular courtyard. Cypress trees flanked the front door.

Jack stopped the car at the front door and turned the key off. He helped Daisy out of the patrol car, climbed with her up the front steps, and pushed the doorbell.

When the door opened, Daisy was surprised. A woman with dark skin in a black uniform, white apron, and cap stood staring at them. Her dark hair, streaked with gray, was pulled back and knotted at the back of her neck. Her eyes darted from side to side under hooded lids.

"Yes? May I help you?"

"We would like to see Miss Giroux about Desmond Walsh." He held up his badge. "I'm Detective Jack Donovan, and this is Daisy O'Malley."

"Do you have any identification besides the badge?" she spoke quietly.

Jack pulled out his driver's license and handed it to her.

"Just a minute." The maid collected it and disappeared, leaving them standing in the opened doorway. She returned within minutes. "Please follow me." She handed Jack his license and led them down the hallway and turned left at the end.

Everywhere Daisy looked, she saw white. To her right, white dining room furniture sat on a white sculpted rug. A large mirror hung above the sideboard. Silver bowls and dishes reflected in the mirror. At the end of the hall, a white railing and steps led to the upstairs. The walls were white, as was a bench near the front door. She stepped on a white shag rug as she followed the maid into the room where Mary Giroux sat in front of a white marble fireplace, with flames from a burning log dancing on the hearth.

She sat at one end of a white brocade chaise longue, leaning on the armrest. Dressed in a white designer pantsuit, she had changed since the funeral. Her legs stretched out on the cushion, with her bare feet barely reaching the opposite end. A long ivory cigarette holder with a burning cigarette dangled between two fingers. In the other, she pressed an ice pack on her forehead. She flicked ashes into the ashtray on the floor next to her. She stared at Jack and Daisy with blue eyes that were red and swollen. Smudged makeup painted her pale cheeks. Her blonde curls were awry. A teacup terrier in her lap stood on all fours and barked.

"Be quiet, Henry." She clamped down on the cigarette holder with her teeth and ran a hand up and down the dogs back. "Please sit." She motioned for Jack and Daisy to the white couch across from her. "You have some questions for me?"

Daisy glanced at the doorway. The maid had quietly left the area. Daisy wondered if she wore felt slippers.

"Yes. I believe I saw you outside Walsh's home the morning of the murder and at the funeral. How long had you known Desmond Walsh?" Daisy asked.

"I've known him for several years. He was the love of my life. I was at home when Charles Miller called me to let me know of Desmond's death. I couldn't believe he was dead. But, when I went to the house and saw them take his dead body, in that horrible black bag, to the coroner's van, I knew it was true."

"Why were you at the murder scene?" Daisy asked.

"Lately, Desmond was pulling away. I was sure I could have changed his mind if I found out why he was acting so strange. I don't know why he was acting that way. He wouldn't tell me even when I begged him and threatened to kill myself." She wiped away a tear that ran down her cheek with the back of her hand. "I called Charlie Miller. I told him I wanted to get the letters I wrote to Desmond before anyone saw them and sold them to the newspapers. Charles was at Desmond's house in the afternoon and asked for them, but Charles told me Desmond wouldn't give them up. He went back later in the early morning before Desmond went to work to see if he could get them and called me. That's when he told me he found Desmond dead."

"Did Charles Miller get any of the letters?" Daisy asked.

"No. When he called me, he said he didn't get any letters. He said when he was searching someone came into the house and he wanted to get out of the house before the police came. He said he left quickly." She sobbed. "I thought maybe he wasn't telling me the truth, and maybe Desmond would give them to me if I begged. I went to his house. The police wouldn't let anyone in the bungalow. Charles said he tried to get inside to search, but the police stopped him. He wasn't allowed into the house. When I saw that no one could get into the house I left."

"Do you know the time he got to the house in the morning?" Daisy asked.

"I don't know." She rubbed her eyes. "Please, don't ask me any more questions. I'm so confused. I can't remember anything." A tear ran down her cheek. She wiped it away with the back of her hand.

"How did you meet Walsh?" Jack asked.

"He was my first director and was pleased with my success in the silent film. He promoted me to one of his prime actresses. Even though there were thirty-five years between us, we became very close. We were going to marry." Tears flowed from her eyes. She looked at Jack. My nightgown is in the closet in his bedroom. Can you get the letters and the nightgown for me? If I don't get those things back and the newspapers find out, my image will be shattered. There's also a locket with his picture in it. It's the only picture I'll have of him."

"I'm sorry. The police have everything. We can't give you anything until the case is over, solved. They may be needed for the trial. We will keep everything until that is over." Jack smiled at her. "They will be under police protection. No one will be able to get their hands on them."

Maybe Miller's the person who knocked me down, Daisy thought.

"We need to interview your mother. Is she here?"

"No, she lives in Venice Beach. My maid will get you her address." She sat up, swung her feet to the side, and set them on the floor. "Rose," she called.

"My sister, Beth, stays with my mother sometimes. Beth is disabled. When she is not with my mother, she lives with a maid in an apartment. She may be with my mother now. She plays the organ in the picture palace in Venice Beach and also visited Desmond. They discussed books. I don't know why, but she's been on the outs with him recently. Beth and I don't always get along. She's jealous of me and tries to tell the press my secrets."

CHAPTER EIGHT

The dog squealed and barked when he fell off Mary's lap.

"Henry, be quiet." Mary leaned over and set the ice pack on the floor. She picked up the dog who stood on his back paws at the side of the chaise lounge.

Daisy smiled, watching the dog curl up on his owner's lap and close his eyes.

"Where is my maid?" Mary leaned over and pushed a button on the wall behind her.

The maid appeared immediately. "Yes, Miss."

"Write down my mother's address, please. Give it to these nice people."

Rose left and reentered the room quickly with a piece of paper. She handed it to Jack.

"Thank you, Miss Miles. We may need some more information and will call you."

"Don't believe the papers. I was the only one Desmond loved. I haven't left the house except for the funeral. Forget what I said about my little sister. She wasn't just a little jealous of me. She was very, very jealous. She resents the attention I get from the public and my mother."

Daisy and Jack stood and started toward the hallway. Jack stopped before they reached the door to the hall.

"Just a minute. Do you own a .38 pistol, Miss Giroux?" Jack asked.

"No. But…"

"But what?" Daisy asked.

"Never mind. I didn't mean to say anything. I'm just not thinking straight. I'm so upset." She lowered her voice to almost a whisper. Her face closed as if she guarded a secret.

"All right. If you can tell us anything else, call me. I'm at the Hollywood police station," Jack said. He took Daisy's arm and followed the maid to the front door. "I guess she doesn't believe or know there were other actresses who thought Desmond Walsh was going to marry them."

"I wondered what she was going to say about the gun. She hesitated when you mentioned it." Daisy asked once they were outside and walking to the car. "Do you think her wide-eyed look of innocence is a smokescreen?"

"Probably. Do you think Miller called from Walsh's house? And that's why the phone was off the hook? He might have been calling her when he heard me shouting at the front door and dropped the phone and hid. He might have been the person who knocked me down."

Walsh's Bungalow

Daisy sat, twisting her earring. *What Would Desmond Walsh's former wife and daughter add to the picture she was getting of this man? Nothing flattering, she was sure.* She glanced at her watch. So far, she was getting mixed messages. She leaned back and closed her eyes.

Jack drove rapidly over side streets.

She couldn't believe she had only been here for two days. So much had happened.

"It's just two o'clock." Daisy stared at the bungalow. *Today it would be called a townhouse.* "It looks much different without the yellow tape over the front door." She threw open the door, ran up the stairs, and pushed the doorbell. She turned to Jack. "This time, the door is closed. It just looks like a home in a nice neighborhood, on a nice afternoon, where nothing bad has happened."

The front doorknob turned. Walsh's former wife, Mrs. Donaldson, opened the door slowly. She stood in the open doorway. Her eyes were unreadable. "Good afternoon, may I help you?" Her brows pulled together in a frown.

Daisy looked into the eyes of a middle-aged woman. Her mousey brown hair hung straight to her ears. Her complexion was pale, and her brown eyes had a bland look. Her dress wasn't particularly stylish and didn't fit well, hanging loosely from her shoulders. Her smile looked pasted on her face. *Very different from the photos of the starlets I saw on the walls the last time I was here.*

"I'm Detective Donovan, and this is Daisy O'Malley." His left eyebrow rose a fraction.

"Oh, I remember." She stood in the doorway for a moment and stared at them. She glanced at her watch. "You are right on time. I'm sorry, I fell asleep waiting for your visit." She took a step back. "Where are my manners? Please come in. The house has been cleaned. Follow me." She led them into the room where the murder occurred.

Daisy heard a crunching noise as she followed.

"Well, I guess they missed some small pieces of glass." Mrs. Donaldson smiled. "I'm sorry."

"Please don't worry. It's always hard to get every piece of the tiny chards that splatter when glass breaks." Daisy glanced around as she entered the room. *The cottage looks beautiful today.* The drapes were open, filling the room with sunlight. All the photos had been removed from the walls, except for the one of President Harding. There was the smell of a meal cooking. She could hear the crackling of a fire on the hearth. "Have you gotten settled, Mrs. Donaldson?"

"Yes. Please. I'm Ethel May. We didn't have many clothes to put away. The kitchen was stocked. My daughter is out for a walk. She should be back soon. I've started a fire to take the chill out of the house. It seems to me it's cool for January in California, but I can say not as cold as New York City." She smiled, leading them across the Oriental carpet.

"We're having a cool winter this year." Jack sat on the chair at the other end of the couch.

"Please sit," she said, lowering herself into the other wingback chairs flanking the couch.

Daisy sat on the sofa next to her. She stared at the ruby cinders around a large log in the fireplace.

"Lieutenant Sullivan told our lawyer the police finished the investigation in the house. Someone cleaned so we could stay here. I don't know how long we'll stay, but I guess until settling the estate. It probably will go fast because the lawyer seems very efficient. I imagine no more than a couple of weeks."

"I saw a piano in the backroom," Daisy smiled. "Do you play?"

"Desmond was the pianist. Music was part of his life." She sighed. "He used to play in the evening, sometimes. I loved to hear him.

Daisy looked around. The room's rug had been cleaned, however, there was a slight discoloration where the blood had pooled. The papers that had been on the desk were gone. *I wonder where they disappeared to.* "There were papers on the desk," Daisy commented.

"They weren't here when we moved in. The desk was empty, as were all the drawers. I imagined the police took everything." She sighed. "Maybe the lawyer has them."

"How did you find out your former husband was deceased?" Jack leaned back in the chair. He watched Walsh's former wife.

"We've been here for a week. We stayed first at the hotel down the street. We moved here after the funeral." She glanced at her watch. "We have only been here for about two hours. Desmond wanted us to meet with his lawyer about his will. He made arrangements for us to come to California. We never got to have a meeting with his lawyer or to sit down with Desmond and the lawyer to see the will. His lawyer notified me about his murder the day it happened."

Daisy leaned forward and listened.

"A neighbor called me. I think it was the woman who talked about the person she saw who left the house the night of the murder. I saw her name in the papers. Desmond told the neighbor and his lawyer to contact me if anything happened to him. They both had the phone number of the hotel where we were staying. When we were contacted about the murder, we came right to the house, but the place was covered with police, people, and the press. So, we decided to go to the lawyer's office. We were going to stay with him and his wife when this place was offered to us." She sighed.

"The lawyer said everything Desmond had, he left to our daughter with me supervising her. After all, she's his blood. She should get everything. I wanted my daughter to see everything in the house before any of his friends came by. I wanted her to be able to keep anything of her father's she wanted and let them have anything she didn't want." She sighed again. "It was almost as if he knew something was going to happen to him."

Daisy noticed a copy of *This Side of Paradise*. The debut novel by F. Scott Fitzgerald laid on the coffee table. It replaced the burned-out candle. *If only she knew how much money her antique shop would get if they had the book and sold it today.*

"Does Desmond have any family in California?" Daisy moved and leaned on the back of the couch.

"I don't believe he does. He came to New York City from Ireland in 1890. If there is any family, they are back in Ireland. I never met them or heard him talk about them."

"How did you meet him?"

"Desmond and I met at a party on Long Island. He always liked the theater and told me he acted in a few plays in Ireland. He also acted in some plays on Long Island. The newspapers gave him lots of praise. After we married, we opened an antique shop. He didn't have time to act." She looked at her hands. "Perhaps that's why he left. He discovered the life he had with antiques wasn't the one he wanted anymore. He wanted the film and theater world." Her expression grew pensive. "Though, to tell you the truth, I always thought he had some kind of mental lapse."

"Was he good at business?" Daisy asked. She turned when she heard the front door thrown open and hit the wall with a thud. The young girl Daisy saw at the funeral stomped into the room.

"This is my daughter, Helen." Ethel May smiled tentatively.

Daisy glanced at the girl wearing men's boots, a long dress, and a long sweater. *She looks like her mother. Except she doesn't smile and looks very angry. She looked nothing like the actresses in the photographs filling the walls of the room when Daisy first saw them.*

"Helen, these people are the police. They are going to help find the person who murdered your father."

"I don't care who murdered him. I don't care about him. I hardly knew my father. To tell the truth, I didn't know him at all." Helen plopped down on the couch. Her brows drew together, and her mouth took an unpleasant twist. "What I knew about him, I read in movie magazines." She picked up her feet and dropped them one at a time on the coffee table with loud thumps. Warning clouds settled on her face. She looked as if she might explode if she had to talk about her father.

"Helen be careful. Get your feet off the table. It's a nice piece of furniture."

Helen didn't move. "It's all junk to me," she sneered.

"I started to tell you about our antique business. We were married in 1901 and opened the shop on Fifth Avenue in the city. Our inventory grew. We started to earn quite a bit of money. I still own the shop."

Daisy smiled. *New Yorkers always refer to New York City as The City, even in 1922. Fifth Avenue is a fancy place for a shop.* "You must have an excellent business."

"Helen was born in 1903. The business did well because we belonged to the yacht club and several other clubs. Desmond made contacts with a lot of the members at all of the clubs. We went to every social event. A lot of the women trusted his ability to furnish their houses. They bought many pieces of furniture from us. The sales went down when he left. Now, many people trust my ability to select the right pieces for them. We make lots of money." Ethel May smiled.

"Mother admit it. He was a womanizer. He flattered all the ladies. That's why they bought from him," Helen butted in.

"Helen, I won't have you talk about your father like that."

Helen set her jaw in a stubborn line. "Fine. I'm going upstairs." Helen dropped her feet to the floor and pushed the table before standing. She clomped to the doorway of the room.

"Wait a minute, Helen," Daisy said. "Your father's valet said he heard your father fighting with a woman in this room a few days ago. When he walked to the doorway of the room, the argument stopped. He said the person was a young girl and was no one he knew. Was that young woman you?"

"Yes, it was me, and yes, we fought. What of it."

"Helen be polite. Why didn't you tell me?" Ethel May's brow creased with worry. Her mouth tightened.

"Mother. It was after we were made aware of the will and traveled here to sign it. He wanted me to stay in Hollywood. I told him I wanted nothing to do with him and wouldn't stay. He kept trying to get me to stay and gave me all the reasons I should. When I finally said I would never stay, he said he might not leave me anything and asked me to leave." She laughed. "I guess I won after all. I guess he didn't have time to cut me out of the will before he got murdered."

Daisy stood listening to what the young girl had to say. She decided Helen was right about one thing. *Desmond Walsh was a womanizer to the very end. All the women at the funeral showed evidence. And a few of them thinking they would marry him.*

"Helen, why didn't you tell me you visited your father and fought with him? How can you be so angry? He was finally trying to make amends."

"You didn't need to know." Helen's eyes lit up. "He was a jerk," her voice was cold. Stains of pink appeared on her cheeks. She stomped to the doorway. "I didn't want you to know. You just wanted his money and would agree with him that I should stay here if you thought you could get your hands on the things he owned and sell them." She glanced at Jack. "I hate this place and want nothing to do with it. I never wanted anything of his. Everything reminds me of how he deserted us. Can I go now?"

"Sure." Jack stared at her.

Daisy watched her go to the doorway and turn the corner as if she was going upstairs. She didn't hear her climb the stairs. *She must be standing in the hallway outside the doorway and listening.*

Ethel May turned a vivid scarlet. "I'm sorry you both had to hear my daughter say the things she did. I'm afraid I have spoiled her. I have tried to compensate for her having no father for so many years." She sighed, trying to hide her embarrassment. "Her father was a man of culture, education, and refinement. Unfortunately, he abruptly disappeared in 1908. We never heard another word from him. I obtained a state decree of divorce in 1912 and married a few years ago."

"Did you know he was in Hollywood?" Daisy asked.

"I thought he was probably dead. In 1918 we were watching a film in a local Picture Palace. When I saw him appear on the screen, I yelled to Helen. "That's your father. I disturbed the others in the audience and told them I was sorry for my outburst. But I saw my husband in the film who I thought was dead. The audience applauded as if I had received an award."

"After we got home, Helen seemed happy and wrote to him in care of the studio. When she didn't get a phone call and never heard from him by letter, she became very bitter. His lawyer told me he made Helen his legal heir in 1918. Desmond must have decided after he got Helen's letter." She pushed herself to a standing position. Her brows drew together. She walked to the doors of the patio.

"I'm such a poor hostess. Can I get you both some tea?"

"No, thank you. Is there anything more you can tell us?"

"No. We will leave after settling the estate. We don't belong in a place like this. The women are so glamorous. We wouldn't fit in." She glanced around the room.

"I never believed he would leave us. As I said before, I thought he had some kind of illness that made him forget about us. I haven't talked to him in years. The first time was last week when we arrived in Hollywood."

Helen stomped into the room. "Mother, you are so naive. He just didn't want a family."

"Helen, go to your room."

Daisy watched the girl turn and glare at her mother.

"We have been together, except for the day she sneaked off and fought with her father. I take a nap in the afternoon. That must have been when she left."

"Well, here's my card." Jack stood, reached into his jacket pocket, and pulled out his card. "If you think of anything that would be of help, please contact me."

"Thank you." Mrs. Donaldson smiled.

Daisy studied the woman. She wondered if Mrs. Donaldson worried her daughter might have slipped out at another nap time and did something to harm her father.

Mrs. Donaldson rose and walked them to the front door. "Goodbye. Thank you for visiting."

Daisy patted her hand. "Things will be all right."

Daisy followed Jack down the front walk.

"Well, I think we can cross them out. Especially the daughter. She's angry, but not a killer," Daisy said.

"You're right. They're just here to collect some things of his to ease their pain and feel he didn't leave them without anything."

"What's on the schedule for tomorrow?" she asked as she slid into the passenger seat.

"Tomorrow morning we'll go to Charlotte Miles in Venice Beach. I'll pick you up at eight. We have to get to her house by boat."

He paused before continuing. "Would you like to have some dinner?" he asked, turning the key in the ignition.

"I think I'll call it a day." She didn't want to say she was still suffering from jet lag. That would start a conversation about how she arrived in Hollywood and when. That was something she didn't want to get explain.

How would she put in plain words that she was from 2018? She was sure he would think she was crazy and wouldn't believe her. He might even take her back to the hospital and have the doctor examine her again.

"I'm going back to the office and read over the statement from Peavey again an. I'll see if the Mounties have found anything about the previous valet, Pryor." He steered the car to the front door of the hotel, parked, and jumped out. He pulled open the passenger door.

"You don't have to walk me in. I can get into the hotel on my own." She didn't want any slip-ups. The man behind the registration desk might bring up something about how and when she arrived. She ran up the stairs.

"You do look beat." He raised his hand and waved. "See you in the morning."

CHAPTER NINE

Daisy looked around. She could smell the faint odor of perfume in the elevator. No one except the operator was there, not even the ghosts. *It must have been from a previous trip.* She felt the bounce of the elevator when it stopped and looked at her feet to make sure it landed even with the reception hall floor. *Everything is okay.*

When she heard Jack's deep voice wish her "good morning," she looked up.

"Good morning, yourself." She glanced at the clock over the reception desk. "You're right on time, as usual."

He handed her a brown paper bag. "I brought you a sweet roll."

"Thank you. A treat like this is just what I need." Reaching for his gift, she smiled.

"I'm parked outside the front door."

"Isn't there a sign out there that says No Parking?"

"The police have certain privileges." He laughed and pushed on the revolving door.

She followed him through the door and to the patrol car. Sliding into the front seat, she unwrapped the sweet roll and took a bite. "This is so good. It's a perfect breakfast. Would you like a piece?" She smiled. "The roll and the icing are filled with sugar, but I love it." She wiped the icing on her lips with her index finger and dug in the brown paper bag for a paper napkin. It took a few seconds for her to rub the icing off. *I need some water.*

"We have a little time before the boats start running to transport people around the Islands. Would you like to stop at a café and have some coffee?"

"No, thanks. Sure you don't want some of the roll before I eat it all?"

"I'm fine. I had a big breakfast."

"Where did you eat?"

"I cooked it."

"You cook?"

"Just because I'm a bachelor doesn't mean I starve. And there's not much damage you can do to bacon and eggs." He laughed.

"Where did you get my treat?"

"Bought it at a bakery near the station."

"You've already been to police headquarters?"

"My dear, my day started at six."

"I was still asleep." She laughed. "Is it a long ride to Venice Beach?"

"No, we're more than halfway there."

"Venice was formerly a saltwater marshland. Now it has four canals that encircle four islands. They are connected by foot bridges. The largest canal is Grand Canal and ends at a large saltwater lagoon. Charlotte Miles lives on this Canal. Her house overlooks the lagoon. After we visit her, I'll take you on a tour of the island and the pier."

"I'd love that. How do the people get around on the island?"

"On foot, bikes, and boats."

"Gondoliers row the tourists around, for a fee. They not only get a view of the area but get serenaded in Italian on the ride. The homeowners use their canoes or boats to navigate the canals and to get to their homes. Near the boardwalk, boats can be rented by visitors if they want to row to one of the houses. Automobiles are just starting to invade the island. They've made a parking lot at the beginning of the Grand Canal," he said, turning into the parking lot. "They're building a bridge that will accommodate cars from the parking lot to Grand Island where Mrs. Miles lives. It's not finished yet." He pointed in front of him. "For now, we'll have to take a boat."

Jack parked next to the path to the boardwalk. He grabbed her hand when she reached his side of the car. "Come on, let's go."

Leaving the boardwalk, she walked, pulling him, down a dirt path lined with palm trees, next to a sloping beach. The sand crunched softly under her feet. Gulls screamed high in the sky.

"Slow down. There's the boatman. It looks as if we're his first customers. It won't take us long to get to the house. There won't be lots of traffic on the water."

A boatman stood next to several rows of boats tied to a dock. Sand covered his high shoes and cuffs of his long pants. A stained white T-shirt showed muscular arms. He chewed on the stem of a pipe.

When they reached him, Jack showed his badge. "Take us to Grand Canal, please. The Mile's bungalow. It's near the lagoon and painted pale blue."

"I know it. It's just a little way around the jetty. Is she all right? Is there some trouble?" the boatman asked through teeth clenched on the stem of his pipe.

"No trouble. We just need to ask some questions about a case. She's all right, I'm sure."

"Oh, are you talking the one in the news? The murder of Desmond Walsh?"

"Have you seen him at her house?"

"I've taken him there a few times."

"Did they seem to get along?"

"I never heard any fighting, but to tell you the truth, I never paid much attention."

The boatman untied the first boat and slid it to the edge of the water.

Daisy slipped into the boat and sat on the wooden seat in the back. The sun beat down.

Jack helped push and jumped in, joining her.

She let the saltwater spray her face. Raising her hand, she shaded her eyes and scanned the island for a light blue cottage.

The boatman rowed around the jetty and headed to their destination.

"There it is." Daisy pointed to a small one-story cottage on her right, surrounded by palm trees and flowering plants. When the boat pulled up to the dock, the boatman leaped out and tied the boat to the dock. He grabbed Daisy's hand and helped her out. She looked at the rising water, walking quickly along the path from the dock to the front of the house. "The tide is coming in. The water is almost to the top of the dock."

"Come back in an hour," Jack said.

"Yes, Sir."

Daisy bounced up the front steps and pushed the doorbell. While it rang, she looked back over her shoulder at Jack. "I wonder what the mother is like."

"You won't have to wait long. She was standing in front of the picture window when we pulled up to the dock."

Daisy heard the tap of leather shoes approach the door.

When the door opened, Daisy stared into the brown eyes of a middle-aged woman. Her dark hair had touches of gray running through it. She had fine lines around her eyes and mouth. "May I help you?" The words came softly out of a full mouth. Her manner was cold and aloof. Daisy stared. *Her body is not as delicate as her daughter's.*

"Mrs. Miles?" Daisy smiled.

"Yes."

Jack stepped forward. "I'm detective Jack Donovan. This is Daisy O'Malley. We would like to ask you some questions about Desmond Walsh. May we come in?"

"Who is it, Mother?" a voice called from the back of the house.

"Don't worry, Beth. It has nothing to do with you."

She offered a square hand to Daisy. "My daughter, Mary, said you were going to stop by. But not when. Please come in." She stood back so they could pass in front of her. Charlotte Miles motioned to them. "I have no idea where my maid is. Please call me Charlotte. Come with me. Sadie will serve us tea on the porch."

"Sadie," she called to her maid. Her voice was calm and impersonal.

Daisy watched Charlotte Miles gesture to the woman in a black uniform over her dark skin. She entered from the back of the cottage, stopped, and stood in the back corner of the room.

"Please follow me." Charlotte nodded to the maid. "Tea please, Sadie."

Daisy looked around the room and followed Charlotte, who led them through a living room to glass French doors. A large front window faced the dock and the lagoon. A navy carpet lay over white tiles which looked like a boarder or the frame of a painting. White rattan chairs with cushions in shades of blue and yellow, and side tables were scattered around the living room. Blue vases holding yellow and white flowers rested on the tables. A large seascape painting hung on the wall opposite the window.

Daisy glanced into a white kitchen as their host led them to a porch. Pink and lavender geometric designed dishes filled the glass-front wall cabinets. Tumblers and wine glasses lined the cabinets next to the dish cabinets. A small gas stove and oven, sink, refrigerator, and a small table with four chairs occupied the room. A plain gray linoleum floor covered the floor.

"May I use your bathroom?" Daisy asked.

"Of course, dear. Behind you, there's a hallway with a bath and two bedrooms. We'll be on the porch." She opened the French glass doors in front of her and led Jack to chairs around a table. She sat with him under a large table umbrella.

Daisy turned and walked to the back of the house. She slid into the first bedroom, decorated with white rattan bedroom furniture. There was a double bed and a bureau with a mirror framed with seashells. She glanced at herself. The breeze on the ride over messed up her hair. She ran her fingers through it and tried to make herself look more presentable. The drapes and bedcovering were lavender with blue flowers. She quickly pulled open the dresser drawers, lifted clothes, and looked underneath them. Finding nothing, she quietly closed the room's door and moved to the next room.

She quickly opened the drawers and searched for anything that might connect Mrs. Miles to the murder. Finding nothing, she quietly opened the clothes closet and scanned the contents. She then flipped through a folder on top of a chair sitting by the door. It had her daughter Mary's name on the cover and several pages of legal papers were inside. She stopped. Hearing a noise outside the room, she closed the folder, dropped it on the chair, and watched the doorknob turn slowly.

The door opened. A girl in a wheelchair pushed herself into the room. "Who are you?"

"I'm Daisy O'Malley. Detective Jack Donovan and I are here to ask your mother some questions about Desmond Walsh."

"I get it. You're searching while my mother is kept busy by the policeman."

"Something like that," Daisy answered while noticing a book on the girl's lap and wanted to change the subject. "*Little Women* is one of my favorite books." Daisy smiled at the girl. "Are you enjoying it?"

"I'm Charlotte's younger daughter. My sister is the actress in the family. I live in an apartment with a woman to help me, but I come here to visit once in a while. My mother hides me and only brings me home when she thinks no one will see me. She's humiliated that she has a daughter in a wheelchair. It must kill her that she didn't know you were coming here today." She laughed. "I saw you come in here. Are you trying to find something to link my sister to the murder of Desmond Walsh? If you tell me, I won't tell anyone."

Daisy didn't know if she could trust the girl, but she kept looking.

"Desmond was dumping her, you know. She was very upset. I was a friend of Desmond. We used to talk all the time. I would get the driver to take me to his house. I played the organ at the Picture Place when they showed one of his movies. He helped me select the right music."

"Did you work with him often?"

"I did, but he was going to replace me. He was becoming to be a bit of a jerk. He was getting sick of my mother trying to run my life. My sister agreed with him. Of course, he was sick of my mother running my sister's life too."

"How did that make you feel that you were being replaced?"

"People gave me standing ovations when I played. I'm angry at all of them. I have a problem, so I couldn't fight with Desmond, but I wanted to get rid of him."

"What is your problem?"

"I can walk. Only Desmond knew I can. I pretend I can't, so I get a little sympathy from my family. My mother never asks the hospital about my condition. The doctors told her I would never walk and were surprised when I finally did. They want the money my mother pays them, so I asked them not to tell. They didn't," she whispered. She leaned towards Daisy. "Please don't tell."

Daisy heard footsteps outside the room. "Who is that?"

"That's Sadie. She's always following me and makes sure I'm well-hidden when we have visitors."

Daisy came eye to eye with the maid when the door opened.

"May I help you?" The maid stood in front of Daisy, blocking the doorway. Trying to slide past the maid, she slithered against the door jam. There wasn't enough room. She was unable to leave.

"Beth, you know you are to keep quiet when we have company." The maid turned and glared at Daisy. "What do you want?"

"I'm sorry. I can't seem to find the bathroom. I thought it might be here next to the first room."

"No, it's the end of the hall." She smiled. "That's how I met this lovely child. We were just having a talk about the book she is reading."

Beth, realizing the maid was distracted, quickly rolled her wheelchair into the maid.

"Beth, you're going to be punished." The maid rubbed her leg.

"Get going," Beth whispered.

Daisy moved to the last closed door and pulled open the door to the bathroom. She stood for a minute.

"They're waiting for you on the porch." The maid limped by.

"I'll only be a moment." Daisy watched the maid walk down the hallway, examining her leg.

"Thank you. I'll be right there." Daisy closed the door. She stood in front of the mirror over a shell-shaped pedestal sink and fluffed her hair, waited a moment, and flushed the toilet. Turning on the faucet, she ran her hands under the water and dried them on one of the blue hand towels hanging on a white, ceramic bar. She quickly pulled open the door to the medicine cabinet. Small, empty envelopes were next to a large plastic envelope with white powder on the lower shelf. She wasn't sure what it was, but she knew it wasn't sugar. Pouring a small amount of the white powder into one of the empty envelopes, she folded it and slipped it into her pocket.

I better get going before the maid shows up again. She hurried to the porch, opened the French doors, and let the doors swing closed behind her. Sitting next to Jack, she looked out over the soft sound of water lapping at the dock. The sun bounced off the spray of the water, sending sparkling droplets of light into the air. She lifted her hand to her forehead, shading her eyes from the sun. Daisy heard the cracking of a branch and looked over Mrs. Miles' shoulder. "Who is the man walking on your lawn?"

"That's Hans. He's my bodyguard and driver." A large man with a bulge in his jacket stopped and looked around the yard. "You can't be too careful in Hollywood."

Daisy was sure the bulge in his jacket was a gun. When she looked again, he was gone.

Sitting beside Jack, she smiled at their hostess and listened to him relay his conversation with Mrs. Miles.

"Mrs. Miles was just telling me her daughter was deeply in love with Walsh and was sure he felt the same about her daughter and wanted to marry her. However, she was not happy about the marriage, because of the difference in their ages. Walsh was more than thirty years older..."

Jack smiled at Daisy.

"This caused some trouble between us." Charlotte continued. "I manage my daughter's career and people say I manipulate her. That's not true. I just keep track of my daughter's acting contracts and earnings. It's true if you've heard, I threatened Walsh to stay away from Mary, but I didn't kill him. I did this when she came to me and was very upset because he told her one day, out of the blue, that he couldn't marry her and gave her no reason. I went to his house and told him to stay away from her. All the ups and downs were distracting her and not good for her career."

"Do you own a gun?" Jack asked.

"…No. I'm deathly afraid of guns. Ask my maid." She pointed to the maid standing in the doorway holding a tray. "Do I have a gun, Sadie?"

"No. No sir. I've never seen Mrs. Miles with a gun. I've never seen one in the house." She looked at the floor as she spoke.

"I didn't threaten him with a gun, I threatened to tell the newspapers about the men at the speakeasies he hangs out with."

Daisy heard the wheelchair rolling toward the porch.

"My mother tells Mary what to do. They're on the outs now. Mary is hiding something. I'm sure of it."

"Beth, go back to your room."

"Mother, tell the truth."

"Please don't pay any attention to her. She likes to make trouble."

"Sadie, please set the tray on the table. I'll pour the tea. Take care of Beth." She looked at Daisy. "Tea, Miss O'Malley? There's milk, sugar, and lemon." She pointed to the tray. "I drink a lot more tea now that we have Prohibition. It replaces my cocktails."

"Just plain, thank you." Daisy reached for the cup and saucer Charlotte handed to her.

Daisy leaned forward. She watched the maid push the wheelchair through the main room.

"Mr. Donovan?"

"No, thank you."

"This is very good. It has a bit of an orange flavor." Daisy waited a moment. She took another sip of tea. Looking through the French doors, she saw the back of the wheelchair going into the hallway. "Do you see your daughter Mary often?" Daisy asked.

"Well, right now, we're having some problems. My daughter thinks I've stolen some of her money. Of course, it's not true. I've had to use some of the money she earned to help her career. She also thinks I'm too possessive." She set her teacup and saucer on the table. "I don't worry about it. We'll work it out. We always do when we disagree. She's young. I have to watch out for her."

"Don't listen to her. She takes all my money, too," Beth yelled. Her voice echoed in the hall.

"Please don't pay any attention to my younger daughter. Sitting in a wheelchair has given her a terrible temperament."

Daisy felt bad for the young girl. Pretending a disability to get attention and living in a dysfunctional family has made her life an unfortunate one.

"Has your daughter Mary been involved with drugs?" Daisy asked.

Mrs. Miles hesitated, then poured herself more tea. "She's had some problems, and I've tried to help her. She's young and beautiful and doesn't realize Hollywood is notorious with predators. She is very impressionable and could get swept up in all kinds of horrible things if I didn't watch her." She took a sip of her tea.

"Well, thank you, Mrs. Miles. If you think of anything else, here's my card. Just call me." Jack stood. He handed her his card.

"Thank you." Daisy smiled. She walked through the living room to the front door of the cottage.

Following Jack down the steps of the front porch, she could see the boatman sitting and puffing on his pipe. Smoke curled in front of his face.

Daisy turned and looked back at the cottage. Beth sat at the picture window.

"Charlotte is hiding something. I saw something that looked like cocaine in the bathroom cabinet and many small plastic bags. I took a sample and put it in one of the empty envelopes for testing. It's in my pocket."

"That's my girl."

Daisy felt her face redden as she slipped the plastic envelope from her pocket and handed it to him.

"Keep it. I'll get it before I go back to the station."

"I also saw legal papers in one of the bedrooms. It looked like Mary is suing her mother."

Jack guided Daisy to the boat. "Back to the boardwalk, please," he said to the boatman.

CHAPTER TEN

When they reached the boat rental dock, Jack tipped the boatman. "Keep an eye on the Miles house for me, will you. Call me at the station if any bad characters show up, or anything unusual happens."

"Will do, detective." He tapped the tobacco from his pipe on the outside of his boot.

"Want a tour of the area?" Jack asked of Daisy.

"I would love it."

"All right let's climb the stairs to the boardwalk. We can stop in a few shops. Business is booming on the pier. There's a great Japanese Tea House. We'll end there for a late lunch."

Daisy looked at the pier. She heard the screams from the roller coaster and other rides.

"Why are those girls in shorts and halters, some with long black stockings, marching from the bathhouse and lining up in front of cameras and people at the long table?"

"It's a bathing beauty contest. The people at the table are the judges."

"Let's wait and see who wins," Daisy said. She was enjoying the warm sun. "Look at that." The winner was a tall, blonde girl with a short curly hair cut. Her face spread into a smile. She was radiant when the judge slipped a ribbon "Miss Venice Beach" over her head.

Today they wouldn't look so happy while they are doing something like it. They would considerate it sexist and not right to judge a woman by her appearance.

"I wanted to take you to the aquarium. It has some of the finest marine specimens on the West Coast. There are a fish hatchery and sea lions at the back of the buildings. However, it looks like rain, so we should stay close to the restaurant," Jack said.

They strolled and looked into shops selling the usual souvenirs of a beach community: towels, t-shirts, things decorated with shells, and many trinkets painted with "Venice Beach." She bought a small hand-painted box with "Venice Beach" inscribed on the top and slipped it into her pocket. *Something to remember my trip into 1922.* Finally, he turned to her. "Getting hungry?"

"Yes, with all the fresh air and only the sweet roll you brought me, I am famished."

"All right let's go back to the tea garden. We should get inside anyway. See the dark cloud appearing in the distance? They are moving in this direction fairly fast."

Daisy stopped and peered over the railing. "What are those men carrying in the boxes? They're going into a tunnel. See them under the boardwalk?"

"They take the boxes filled with bootleg alcohol to the hotels, restaurants, and speakeasies. It's smuggled in from ships that can't come in close to the shore because the water is too shallow. Small rowboats unload the alcohol from the big ships in the Pacific Ocean and bring it in. They can only smuggle it at low tide. At high tide, some of the tunnels get water into them. The water wets the sand and makes it hard to walk with heavy boxes. The men who deliver the alcohol sink into the sand. Some of the tunnels they use are next to dirt roads. The bootleg liquor can also be loaded onto trucks on the roads and then distributed around California and other nearby states."

Daisy heard music. "Where's the music coming from?"

"It's from the dance hall next to you."

She peeked into the doorway of the building. A small group of musicians played from a stage while couples danced around the large room. Sconces along the walls provided dim light. She stared. The man and the woman from the hotel danced in the back of the large dance floor. She caught their eye and waved.

"Do you know someone in there?"

"Not really. I thought I saw someone I met at the hotel. I'm sure I'm wrong." *I don't want him to go in and try to meet them. How would I explain why he couldn't see them?*

Daisy grinned. She saw women collecting tickets as men asked them to dance. *If I remember the dance places where that happened were called Taxi-dances.*

"Here we are."

She looked at the building that was a replica of a Japanese house.

"I can smell the spices." She peeked in the door. "We just made it. I can feel raindrops." Daisy ducked through the restaurant door.

"You'll enjoy the food. They'll serve you small portions of fish, meats, and vegetables. You'll get tastes of many different Japanese dishes."

She looked around the restaurant. Colorful Japanese lanterns were strung around the room. Small vases with flowers had been placed on each table. Soft Oriental music played in the background.

"Let's order a number ten. It's for two people. We'll get a group of the best dishes. Is warm Saki okay?"

"Yes."

"After lunch, I'm going to take you back to the hotel. We're going to a speakeasy tonight so dress up. I'll pick you up at nine."

Prison visit

Daisy laid on the bed, deciding if she should get under the covers and take a nap. The saki had made her tired. Surprised when the phone rang, she sat up and propped her back against the decorative pillows.

"Hello, Jack." She listened to his voice.

"Our plans have changed. Lieutenant Sullivan got a phone call from the warden at Greenville prison near Sacramento. One of the prisoners has some news about the murder of Desmond Walsh."

"Okay, when do we leave? I'll be ready in about twenty minutes."

Hanging up the phone, she was wide awake and raring to go. She ran down the stairs to the first-floor gift shop. "This is going to be interesting," she whispered. "I guess the speakeasy is on hold for now."

The salesgirl smiled. "Did you ask me something?"

"No, I was talking to myself."

"May I help you?"

"I need to pack for an overnight trip to Northern California." She looked around. "I'll take that brown bag. Just put it on my bill. You don't have to wrap it." Daisy grabbed it and ran. She took the stairs two at a time. She was surprised to find her door wide open. She stood in the doorway. "He asked if I wanted to take a road trip. Of course, I do," she whispered as she looked around her room for an intruder. "Thank goodness. No one is here. Not even the ghosts. Though ghosts could come in without an open door. I have to be more careful, even if I'm in a hurry."

Packing didn't take her very long. She grabbed the tag and tore it off the bag and packed a change of clothes, toothbrush, paste, and makeup. Locking the door, she headed to the elevator. She heard music and looked up. Desmond Walsh and his blonde friend waved. "Sorry, don't have time to talk." She laughed. They were already gone.

"That was fast." Jack took her bag.

"You were fast, too."

"I cheat. I keep a bag in the trunk of my car. I get calls like this every once in a while. Let me have yours."

They ran down the stairs of the hotel. Jack tossed her bag in the backseat of his patrol car and slammed her door shut after she slid into the passenger seat.

Once they got out of the city and auto fumes, Daisy opened her window and enjoyed the cool fresh air. She looked at the scenery. "The rocky coast is beautiful." She was so surprised by the differences between the north of California and the southern part of the state. Large trees grew on the edge of the rocky shores. Towns were spread out. Farms and fields filled a lot of the land. There was no congestion, like in Los Angeles.

"Where are we going to stay?"

"We'll be in the small town of Greenville in a guest house. It's a beautiful old Victorian house. A retired couple made it into a wonderful place to stay overnight when visiting northern California. They do a good business with tourists and families of the prisoners. I've stayed there before. The prison is outside the city limits."

Daisy made small talk as she watched the scenery. Soon she saw a sign for Greenville. "The sign says, Greenville, population 1000. You're right. It is a small town." Daisy stared out of the window. "There's the prison. It looks like a medieval building with its granite walls and tower. The only thing they didn't have in medieval times was razor wire."

Jack glanced at his watch. "It's almost dinner time, and the owner is an excellent cook. I know you'll enjoy dinner. We'll go to the prison tomorrow morning." He parked in front of the house, grabbed the bags, and walked to the front door.

"Do a lot of the town's people work at the prison?" she asked, staring at the house. It reminded her of her home in Maine.

"I would probably say half the town has something to do with the prison. Besides guards, there are cleaning persons, carpenters, and some of the farmers supply vegetables and fruit," Jack said.

Daisy heard the song "Toot Tootsie Goodbye" play when Jack pressed the doorbell.

A plump woman answered the door. Her skin was like peach-tinted cream. White-as-snow hair framed her face. "Good evening, Detective Donovan, and you must be Daisy O'Malley. I'm Mrs. O'Hara." She extended her hand. Daisy felt its warmth.

"Yes." Daisy smiled.

"Please come in. My husband will be home shortly. He's a guard on the day shift at the prison." Her lips broke into a wide smile. There was a sparkle in the deep, blue eyes that met Daisy's. "I'm sorry for the apron. I was just baking rolls for dinner." She took a handkerchief from the apron pocket and dabbed her forehead.

"Your rooms are ready." Untying her apron and draping it over her arm, she led them up a circular staircase. "They're at the top of the stairs. Your room is on the left, Detective, and yours is right across from him, Miss O'Malley. Cocktail time is in the living room in an hour."

Jack opened the door to his room. "See you in a little while, Daisy."

Daisy gasped when the owner opened the door to her room. "It's beautiful." She felt she was in another time. *And I am.* A duvet and canopy in a small floral-patterned material covered the canopy bed. All the furniture was from the Victorian age. She stared. *I'm closer to the Victorian age now than I am in my own time. No wonder the room is furnished like it is. The Victorian era wasn't so long ago.* She quickly hung up her clothes, washed her hands, and ran a brush through her hair. She opened the door of her room, turned to the stairs, just as Jack left his room.

"I love this place." *It probably isn't around anymore.* She ran her hand down the highly polished stair railing.

The owner offered them a glass of sherry when another couple joined them. When the other guests found out why Jack and Daisy were in Greenville, they admitted they read about the murder in their local newspaper. They asked questions about the crime from the time they went in to dinner until the owner suggested they go back to the living room and have coffee.

Daisy, tired of discussing the case, excused herself. "I think I'll turn in early. I'm going to skip the coffee and do some reading." She smiled at Mrs. O'Hara. "Dinner was delicious."

"Thank you. The library is behind the staircase. Breakfast starts at eight," the owner said.

Daisy stopped in the library, picked up a book on the history of California, and climbed the stairs to her room. She heard steps following her and turned when she reached the top of the stairs. Jack stood, watching her.

"I grabbed a book when you started up the stairs."

"Let's see what you're going to read." She pulled on the book in his hand so she could see the title. "A mystery. Don't you get enough at work?"

"I'll probably fall asleep before I finish the first chapter." He laughed.

"I needed to get away from the questions. I couldn't stand talking about the case anymore. See you at breakfast." She smiled, opening her bedroom door.

"Sleep well." Jack waved. "I think we'll skip the sit-down breakfast. We'll just grab a roll and cheese and fruit. Bring your suitcase. We'll go back to Hollywood from the prison." He threw the words over his shoulder.

"Sounds good."

Greenville Prison

"Jack Donovan from Hollywood. We're here to meet with the Warden and a prisoner." Showing his badge to the guard at the gate, Jack waited while the gate guard scanned the logbook.

"Yup. You're on the list. Go right through. He's expecting you. His office is the last brick building on the left." The gate swung open, and the guard waved them on.

"This is creepy. There are prisoners all over the place. They're in black and white striped uniforms. The guards are standing everywhere in the yard. Look. They're walking on the wall too. There's a machine gun in the tower." *This place goes on and on. It's huge.*

All of a sudden, she heard a loud alarm. Guards ran with guns and herded the prisoners into buildings. She heard the bars of cells slam shut.

"There's the warden's building." He pulled up and parked. "Get out, run, and ring the doorbell to the right of the door."

Daisy ran with Jack. Her hand shook as she pushed on the bell. A voice came back to her.

"Whose there?"

"It's Jack Donovan and Daisy O'Malley."

"Get in here quick." The warden shoved open the door.

Daisy felt as if a hand closed around her throat. She pushed through the door with Jack. It swung shut immediately.

The Warden greeted them. "Come into my office."

"What happened?"

"Three convicts high-jacked the prison train we use to move materials. They smashed through the front gate of the prison. We caught them right away, and they're in solitary now, but the prison is still on lockdown for a final check of all the cells. We have to make sure we have every prisoner accounted for."

"We were just there." Daisy sighed with relief. "Things were over so quickly."

"You'll have to wait until things settle down to do your interview. It won't take long. Can I offer you some coffee?"

"I would love some," Daisy sat and took a cup from the Warden.

"Sugar and cream," he asked.

"No, thank you. Just black." Tasting, she was surprised it wasn't too bad.

Another siren rang, "What's that?" Daisy asked.

"The "all clear" siren."

"It's okay now. You can meet the prisoner in the conference room adjacent to my office. There's a long table and chairs. I'll have the prisoner brought in. Go on in and wait."

Daisy watched the prisoner cleaning the Warden's office moved close to the door of the conference room. He looked at them and slowed down his cleaning. He scrutinized the furniture. She noticed he kept going over the same pieces of furniture with his dust rag.

Daisy slid a chair from the wall into the middle of the table. She watched Jack pace. Within a few minutes, the clang of shackles and the shuffle of soft-soled shoes made her look toward the doorway. Her heart pounded. A flicker of apprehension ran through her.

The prisoner stared at Daisy. "Well, well. Hello Miss. Alfonso Caruso. I didn't know a pretty lady would be here."

The guard pushed Caruso into a chair at the end of the table. He stood with a frown behind Caruso in the doorway with his feet apart and held a rifle in his arms.

"Okay, Alfonso, what is it you have to tell us about the murder of Desmond Walsh?" Jack asked.

"First, don't be in such a hurry. I need something for the information I'm giving you."

"Like what?" Jack's voice was bland.

"Let's see… Early parole. Maybe something more. I'll have to think about it."

"What are you in for?" Jack's voice was terse. Annoyance hovered in his eyes.

"Twenty years for bank robbery."

"Well, let's see what you have to give us. We have to corroborate it."

"I'm thirsty. Can I have some coffee?"

Daisy peeked into the warden's office. The man was cleaning close to the doorway.

"Wait a minute. Are you going to give us some information?"

"I think I deserve a good cup of coffee, not that stuff they serve in the cafeteria."

"Okay, guard, give him a cup."

The prisoner sighed with happiness, taking a long drink. "This is good."

"All right. Now tell us something."

The prisoner leaned forward and whispered. "Well, I heard it's someone in the Mafia. Maybe even Capone."

"Okay, we'll check it out and get back to the Warden."

Daisy looked through the open door for the prisoner who was cleaning. He was gone.

The guard tapped the prisoner on the shoulder. "Okay, Alfonso. Anything else?"

"Not right now." He glanced at Jack. "I'll be waiting to hear from you."

"Back to your cell." The guard frowned.

Jack led Daisy to the Warden's office. "Thank you. We'll get back to you after we do some checking." He turned to Daisy. "It's going to be hard to catch a Mafia person and get him to take the blame. If we do, it will be hard to convict him."

"Charles Miller's name never came up. Did it?"

"No, it didn't."

They made small talk on the way back. Daisy wondered if Alfonso was telling the truth. She still thought Charles Miller had something to do with the murder and had ties to the Mafia."

She saw the sign for Los Angeles. "Why does the trip back always seem shorter?"

He smiled. "I want to stop at the station for a second before I take you to your hotel. Do you mind?"

"No, it's fine. I'll wait in the car. I'll start reading the book I borrowed from the B& B."

"What's the book?"

"*This Side of Paradise.* F. Scott Fitzgerald's debut book. I thought it would be more interesting than a history book. I told Mrs. O'Hara I would mail it back to her. Have you read it?"

"Yes. Most of the characters were drawn from Fitzgerald's life."

"I'm having fun figuring out which friend he is writing about."

He pulled up to the curb at the police station. "I'll be right back."

"That was quick," she said when Jack returned. "I just got to the last page of chapter one.

"Sullivan had some bad news." Jack frowned.

"What happened?"

"We will probably never know if Alfonso was telling us the truth."

"Why?"

"He was killed, knifed to death, a half-hour after we left the prison. The word snitch was written in his blood next to him. The Mafia has a code of silence,

'Omerta.' Death, if someone cooperates with the police."

"Maybe we can get some information at the speakeasy tonight."

Jack pulled his patrol car to the front of the hotel. "Pick you up at nine."

"See you then." Daisy slammed the car door and ran into the hotel. "I hope I see the ghosts, and they tell me if we're getting close."

CHAPTER ELEVEN

Night at a Speakeasy

Daisy stood in front of the open closet. She pulled the peacock blue dress off its hanger and held it up in front of her. Glancing in the mirror over the dresser, she thought for a moment. *No. I think it will be the black dress with sequins tonight.* She returned the dress to the closet, pulled out the black one, and tossed it on the bed. She bent down, picked up her black, t-strap shoes with two-inch heels, and placed them on the floor in front of the bed. Opening the top drawer of the dresser, she took the black silk headband with side feathers and black undergarments.

I think I'll take a nap. It's going to be a late night. She picked up the phone's receiver and dialed the front desk. "Please call me at seven. Thank you." She put the phone beside her on the bed, pulled the chenille throw to her shoulders, and closed her eyes.

A loud ring woke her. She sat straight up and stretched her hand to the bedside table. "Where is it? Oh." She felt the bed. Knocking the phone off the receiver, she put it up to her ear and listened. "Yes. Thank you." *That was fast. It seems as if I just closed my eyes.*

"A shower is just what I need." She slid off the bed, ran into the bathroom, climbed over the side of the tub, and started the shower. Jumping when the cold water hit her, she bent and peered at the faucet. *I turned the wrong one.* With a turn of the hot water knob, she let the mix of hot and cold-water flow over her. She thought about her adventure into the 1920s and how much she missed her home and daughter in Maine. A tear ran down her cheek. *Come on, Daisy. This case will be solved soon, and I'll be on my way home.* She turned her thoughts to the night ahead.

She was looking forward to seeing the party atmosphere of 1922 and how people survived Prohibition. When the bath water cooled, she slid over the side of the tub. She pulled a towel from the rack beside the tub and dried off. She strolled into the bedroom with the towel wrapped around her. *I should have bought a bathrobe.* She stood in front of the dresser mirror and reached for her cosmetics kit and applied her makeup carefully, wanting it to be perfect.

She dressed slowly in the black sequined flapper dress. She glanced at her hair. Trying to decide what to do with it, she thought for a moment. *Okay.* She pulled it back and fastened it with a gold clip, letting tendrils fall around her face. Looking at her reflection in the mirror, she smiled. *I don't look too bad in twenties clothes.* Finished, she glanced at her watch. It's eight fifty-five. By the time I get downstairs, it will be nine. She closed the door to her room, locked it, and started to the elevator. She could hear "*Five Foot Two, Eyes of Blue*" coming from somewhere in the hallway.

"Ghosts again, but this time happy ones." She was getting used to seeing ghosts and wasn't surprised when she looked and saw a couple dancing down the hall. *It's a different couple. One I haven't seen before here in the hotel, but I'm sure I saw them at the dancehall in Venice Beach. They danced next to Desmond and his date.* "I saw you at the dance hall in Venice Beach," she called to them. "Say hello to Desmond Walsh."

"We go to the pier often. So does Desmond. We'll say hello for you." They answered before they disappeared into the wall at the far end of the hallway.

"Guess I'll have to operate the controls. There is no one here to give me a ride. Let's see, pull the crank to the left, and I'll go down." She closed the gate, turned the crank, and smiled. "One day, I'll get those ghosts to speak to me and say more than a few words."

The elevator landed with a bounce. She looked down and saw the car stopped one inch from the floor. She stepped out of the elevator and tripped. *I'm so bad at operating this thing. I would never get a job as an elevator operator.* Heading to the reception desk, she felt a breeze. A whistle of approval surprised her. She glanced at Jack and smiled.

Jack pushed through the revolving door. His tux fit well. His hair was still damp from a shower. As he approached, his aftershave lotion reached her nose before he did. He smelled very masculine.

"You clean up pretty well yourself."

Jack laughed, put his arm around her waist, pulled her to him, and hugged her. "We'll walk. It's warm tonight."

"Where are we going?"

"We passed it yesterday when we went for lunch. It's next to the restaurant."

"I didn't see the door."

"That's the secret. It's hidden in the wall, and it looks like it is part of the restaurant."

"Now…I remember hearing music when we reached the restaurant."

"The speakeasies are well-hidden, so the police have trouble getting in and raiding the places before the clients escape to a place the police can't catch them. Plus, the owner has an employee standing on the roof. He watches for the police and flashes a light when he sees them getting close. There are usually tunnels under the speakeasies for the people to hide in or run through. They get to streets far enough away so no one can connect them with the speakeasy." Jack looked around. "In this one, there is also a bookcase that swings open. The patrons can get into a room behind it and hide. Some of the speakeasies look like legitimate businesses. No one knows what is happening in them. Three blocks from here, there is a lamp company that sells only to special patrons. If you know someone and can get in, you won't see a lamp anywhere. Another near here is a dry cleaner. The racks of clothes never change," Jack said.

"Why did they start speakeasies?" Daisy asked.

"They were started to avoid tax on the alcohol they smuggled in when they were breaking the eighteen amendment. The owners pay very high rents because they might have to vacate without warning and never come back. The bartenders take the brunt of the arrest if the police find the speakeasy, but it's a good job because they're paid well and paid if they go to jail. They get a bonus when they get out of jail."

Jack stopped in front of a paneled wall next to the front door of the restaurant. He pushed on a button in the wall at the level of a doorknob.

Daisy was surprised. A small piece of the wall at the height of Jack's shoulder slid back.

He leaned forward and whispered something. She assumed it was a code word only special people knew so they could get in. The wall swung open. His hand grabbed her arm and pulled her into a stairwell before the door groaned closed. She heard smooth jazz playing.

"We go down. The light is dim on the stairway, so be careful."

She looked down at well-worn steps and moved carefully.

Her stomach flip-flopped. She was on her way to a speakeasy and a new adventure. A few minutes later, another door slid open. She stood in a smoke-filled room.

Jack guided her to a bar where groups of men and women stood. Some held their drinks and looked as if they nursed black moods. One group drank tall beverages and cocktails and talked and laughed with each other. Others chugged the bootleg liquor from a bottle. Small café tables with two chairs were scattered around the room. Red padded couches with low tables in front lined mirrored walls. The smooth jazz turned into dance music. Several couples standing at the bar moved to the middle of the floor and began to dance.

Daisy searched the room and studied the faces of the men. "Charles Miller isn't here."

"You're right. Perhaps he'll show up soon."

Daisy stared at the black man standing on a small stage, playing the trumpet. He wiped his forehead with a white handkerchief between songs. "I know who that is."

Jack turned and gazed at her. "Who is it?"

"…Louis Armstrong." She left out "a young" Louis Armstrong.

"Have you been to a speakeasy before?"

"No. I've just heard about him." She sighed with relief when she saw a man approaching them. He distracted Jack from asking any more questions about her knowledge of Louis Armstrong.

"Jack. Who is this beautiful woman you're with?" the man asked, taking his cigar from his mouth. There was a long moment of silence.

"Lucky, let me introduce you to my friend Daisy." He smiled. "Daisy, Lucky Luciano."

"What are you doing here, Lucky?"

"I had some work to do here in Hollywood." He laughed. "We just had a snowstorm. I had to get warm."

"I just came in from the Big Apple. And Daisy, the Big Apple is the nickname for New York City. It has nothing to do with fruit. It means a major prize money in horse racing."

"How do you do, Mr. Luciano?" She extended her hand.

"Please, Lucky." He took her hand. Bending, he kissed her fingers tips. "The drinks are on the house," Lucky yelled, turning to the bartender. He took a drag from his cigar and slowly blew the smoke out.

Daisy forced a smile and withdrew her hand. The smell of the cigar made her nose burn, and her fingers felt damp. There were no napkins on the bar. She had all she could do not to wipe her fingers on her dress.

The bartender, reading her mind, handed her a wet rag from behind the bar.

She flashed a smile of thank you.

"That's okay, Lucky. I'll pay." Jack's jaw clenched. "Tell me. You haven't had anything to do with a prisoner at Greenville Prison, have you?"

"No. I don't know what you're talking about. Where's that prison?"

"You'll find out Lucky if you get caught and convicted for getting involved in illegal business here in California."

Lucky took a long drag on his cigar. "You won't let me pay?" His eyes narrowed.

"No, thanks," Jack said.

Daisy heard Lucky whisper something as he walked away. Her eyebrows shot up. Her expression grew serious.

Jack signaled to the bartender. "White wine and a scotch, Chives Regal." He leaned toward Daisy.

"No white wine tonight," the bartender leaned over and whispered. "The police captured our last shipment before it got to our warehouse."

"I thought the police looked the other way," Daisy said.

"They do most of the time, but there was a group of women outside the hiding place with signs against the evils of alcohol, so they had to fine us. They smashed the bottles."

"How about drinking what I'm having?" Jack turned to her.

"That's fine. Put a little water in mine... What did Lucky say as he walked away?"

"He said 'someday'." Jack laughed.

"What does that mean?" she asked, accepting the glass of scotch the bartender handed her.

"He's big in organized crime in New York City and visits here a lot in the winter. He thinks if I let him pay, I'll owe him, and the next step will be that I'm on my way to being corrupted." He glanced at Lucky standing at the bar. "With prohibition, there is lots of criminal activity. Organized crime, the Mafia, supplies a lot of the booze. Organized crime has infiltrated labor unions, and all kinds of businesses. Gambling, drugs, and prostitution. Most of the politicians and police are paid off. If a case of murder comes to trial, witnesses and jury members are bribed with money or threatened with death. They're afraid to testify. He's hoping someday I join the corruption."

A sudden cold knot formed in her stomach. She realized how the Eighteenth Amendment helped bring Mafia corruption to the United States.

"Lucky is always trying to get me to take a bribe. So I don't even let him pay for my drinks. He's head of one of the New York City five families, but he comes to California often and always brings trouble with him."

"Walsh hung out here once in a while. As you know, he got information for his work with the government. He was trying to stop the flow of drugs infiltrating this country. Hollywood has a big problem. Some people think the Mafia might have murdered him."

"The man at the prison gave us the name Capone. Is he here tonight?" She watched him look around the room. "So, do you hang out here often?"

"No. I just come in occasionally to see who is here. I listen to conversations to find out what is going on." He smiled. "Come on, let's sit at a table." Holding onto her elbow, he guided her to a small café table.

A few minutes after they sat, a blonde-haired woman with very red lipstick that matched her red dress, came over to the table and sat on Jack's lap.

Biting her lip, Daisy looked away. However, she listened to their conversation. She was glad the light in the room was dim, and it hid the flush in her cheeks.

"Hello, Jackie." The girl put her arm around his neck and leaned her head on his shoulder. "I've missed you. It's been weeks since you've been here." She ran her fingers through his hair. "You've missed a lot."

Daisy's dismay grew, and she became more uncomfortable by the minute. Her hands twisted nervously in her lap. She regarded his friend with curiosity, wondering how he felt she compared to the woman in his lap. She came back to reality. *It doesn't matter what he does or who he does it with. The dreadful fact is I have to keep reminding myself I come from another time.* She watched Jack untangle himself.

"Stella, this is Daisy. Daisy, Stella."

Stella smirked as she said, "Hello." Quickly turning her back on Daisy, she nuzzled Jack's neck.

Angry at herself for feeling embarrassed, Daisy forced a stiff smile. "Hello. It's nice to meet you." She leaned toward the woman. There was a sourness in the pit of her stomach. *Stop Daisy. You're just here to help solve the murder. Why am I getting annoyed?* Her lips thinned with irritation.

"Jack, Al Capone is in the back room. He's visiting from Chicago. When you're alone, we can get together with him." Stella kissed him on the cheek.

"That would be great, Stella."

Daisy heard Jack's name yelled again. She looked around. An overweight man belonging to the voice walked toward their table.

"Jack. Nobody told me you were here."

"Al, I just got here. When did you get into town?"

"Just about an hour ago. It's cold in Chicago at this time of the year. The wind coming off Lake Michigan is not good. I needed to warm up."

Daisy watched Capone. He was a short figure with a round face, in a shiny, dark gray suit, chewing on a cigar. He inhaled smoke from the cigar and blew smoke into the air when he stood next to them.

Daisy coughed and backed away from him. She raised her hand and covered her mouth and nose.

He grabbed her hand with his fat, damp fingers. "And who is this?"

"Daisy O'Malley. Daisy meet Al Capone."

Like Lucky, he pulled her fingers to his lips and kissed them. And like her reaction to Lucky, she had the desire to wipe her fingers.

"Why are you in Hollywood, besides to get warm? Any contact with someone in prison up north?" Jack didn't mince words. He got right to the point.

"What are you talking about? I'm here to do some business with the restaurant union and to enjoy the warm weather. I had too much celebrating with my family during the holidays and needed a rest.

"Jack, you know I only have contact with the people around Los Angeles. Come and see me before you leave tonight."

Daisy watched him wander off.

Ignoring Stella, she looked at Jack. "What about Capone? What's his story?"

"He was from a good family but got in with a bad bunch of men. After working his way up in the Chicago crime family, he decided he loved the life of crime and never left it."

Jack heard his name called and turned. The bartender held up the phone in Jack's direction.

"See you later, Stella." He almost dumped her on the floor as he got up.

Stella righted herself and slid onto the empty chair. She leaned over and whispered to Daisy. "Are you new in the department?"

"No, I just met Jack at the Walsh murder and somehow have ended up helping with the investigation." Daisy chewed on her lower lip.

"Be careful. He is a good investigator but takes lots of chances."

"Are you?" Daisy stopped.

Stella looked around to see who was near them. "Yes. I'm with the District Attorney's Office. This is my cover. Remember, be careful." She got up from the chair and wandered to the bar.

"You too," Daisy said as Stella left. She thought about what might happen if Stella's cover was exposed, how she might end up in a desolate field and suffer a horrible death with her body hidden forever.

She saw Jack returning to the table.

"What was the phone call?" She saw Al Capone edge closer to them.

Jack leaned forward. "I'm afraid it's Charles Miller. Sorry to cut the evening short. We have to go." He took Daisy's arm. "We won't be interviewing him anymore."

She watched as Capone inhaled his cigar and smiled as he slowly slipped away.

"What happened to him?"

"He's been murdered."

CHAPTER TWELVE

Venice Beach

"Let's get my car."

She moved quickly. "Where are we going?" Daisy asked as she slid into the passenger seat. "I guess I don't have time to go back to the hotel and change."

"No. I have a jacket in the trunk. You can put it on. He lives in the same neighborhood as Walsh's house, but they found him on Venice Beach."

"At Venice Beach. Do they know why he was there?"

"No. He was in one of the rental boats. His car was on the road next to the tunnels leading from the beach to the basement of a hotel. In the car, there was a note with the time 12:30 a.m. written on it. There's an opened box in the back of the car. It's empty. Whatever he had in there, is now gone."

"How was he killed?" she asked, walking with Jack.

"A gunshot to the head. No gun was found. A preliminary exam at the scene shows there's a question of him knowing his murderer."

"I'm sure Capone heard you say Miller had been killed. He didn't seem too surprised. He looked pleased."

Jack jumped out of the car and parked when he reached the boardwalk. He ran to the back of the car and grabbed his jacket out of the trunk. Joining Daisy, he put it around her shoulders.

Daisy slipped out of her shoes when she reached the sand. Holding them by the straps, she swung them as she followed Jack. Her feet sunk into the sand. "Who found him?" she asked, slipping on the jacket when they reached the scene of the murder.

"One of the sailors who was delivering bootleg whiskey to the hotel went to the boats to have a cigarette before he rowed back to the ship in the Pacific. He found the body lying on the steering wheel of the boat."

"It's strange." Daisy stared at the scene. "He seemed to be talking to someone sitting next to him when he was shot." She got closer to the boat and turned to Jack. "Look at him. He's turned sideways in his seat. His head is laying sideways in the sand. The sand is soaked with blood."

"The tide is coming in. It will fill this area in a little while. Whoever murdered him didn't want him found. They hoped the body would wash out to sea at high tide and never be found."

"Well, that didn't happen."

Daisy heard the noise of car wheels sliding to a stop in the sand behind her. She glanced over a shoulder. "The coroner is here." She watched the coroner and his assistant park on the dirt road near the tunnel then struggled with pushing the stretcher on the sand the short way to the boats and the body.

"What's the white powder on his jacket?" the coroner's assistant asked, glancing down at the body.

"It looks like cocaine," Jack said.

"That reminds me, I never gave you the powder I found at Mrs. Miles' place," Daisy whispered.

"I'll get it when we get back to the hotel."

"Do you think the murder is connected with Desmond Walsh's murder?"

Jack thought for a minute. "I don't think he had anything to do with Walsh's murder. However, he was a big shot in the film industry. He might have known who committed the murder. A manager at Paramount Pictures would know a lot of dirt on a lot of people. One thing being, all of the people with drug problems. He owed money to the Mafia, so he had a connection to Capone and Lucky."

"Perhaps, he was blackmailing one of the people he knew had a drug problem and was using the money to repay a debt to the Mafia, and they didn't want to pay him. To make sure he would stop blackmailing them, they made sure he ended up dead," Daisy said.

Jack called the coroner. "How long do you think he's been dead?"

"Not long. You'll have all the information after the autopsy. By the appearance of the bruises on his face, he must have been beaten sometime before he was murdered. I can tell you the person was about a foot away from him when he or she fired the shot." The coroner and his assistant slid the body into the black bag, zipped it, and strapped it to the stretcher. They struggled to push the stretcher through the sand, lifting it at times.

Jack walked over to them. "Let me." He helped them with the stretcher until they got to the dirt road and the van. He waved to the coroner. "Will call you in a while to see what you found."

He turned, joining Daisy. "Let's go to the hotel and see if he was on his way to meet someone."

Daisy trudged through the sand as she followed Jack to the steps leading to the boardwalk and the hotel. "Wait a minute." She sat on a step and slipped on her shoes.

When they reached the hotel, he stood back, letting Daisy push through the revolving door of the hotel and followed.

She waited for him, and they walked side-by-side to the reception desk.

He took a deep breath and showed his badge to the desk clerk. "I want to speak to the hotel manager. Is he in the back?" Jack started toward the hall behind the reception desk.

"Just a minute, sir… You can't just barge in there. The manager is on a long-distance phone call. You can wait on the bench in the hallway outside his office. I'll contact him and let him know you're waiting for him." He picked up the phone on the desk and relayed the message.

Jack paced back and forth, working off excess energy as he waited. He stopped and turned to the front desk when he heard the desk clerk call him.

"You have a phone call, detective."

Daisy watched Jack as he listened to the voice on the other end of the phone.

"Thanks." He walked back to Daisy. "That was the coroner. A preliminary finding is that the gun that killed Miller was a .38. The same caliber that murdered Walsh."

"Well, think it was the same person?"

"Probably." He was quiet and began to pace again as they waited.

Daisy wanted to ask him more questions. He looked so deep in thought she didn't want to disturb him.

Daisy stared at the family, walking toward the reception desk. She realized the woman heard Jack's comment.

A man and woman with two little children stood at the desk. The woman held the children's hands, who were trying to escape, while the man started to register.

"What, what's going on? Who was murdered? Harvey let's get out of here," the woman yelled. She let go of the children's hands. "Stay right next to me."

Daisy was surprised they didn't move.

The clerk looked at her. "This trouble with the police has nothing to do with the hotel. Everything is fine. There was no murder in the hotel. Something happened on the boardwalk. The police just want to know if a stranger came through the lobby. Whoever they're looking for hasn't come in here, and we've heard nothing."

"All right, if you're sure?" She sighed. "We have a reservation. Mr. and Mrs. Prichard." She turned quickly. "Harvey, let's get to our room, sign in, and grab the suitcases and key. And hurry up. Children, give me your hands and don't let go." She grabbed the children and ran to the elevator. Her husband slipped the key into his jacket and followed, struggling with their suitcases.

Before the elevator door opened, the little boy turned and stared at Daisy. He pointed in her direction. "Look at the man. He's all dirty."

The mother squinted. "Dicky, there's no one there. Come with me. We're going to our rooms. Don't make stories up." She pulled him close to her.

The little boy began to cry. "I'm telling the truth."

Daisy looked at the registration desk. Desmond Walsh stood at the desk. "That young boy will realize someday he has a wonderful gift," Daisy whispered. "Though his mother might make his life miserable about what he sees. I hope he doesn't hide his abilities."

The mother pulled her children to her. "If we see anybody lurking around, we'll tell you immediately," she yelled over her shoulder.

The door to the back room opened. "Can I help you, Detective?" The man at the reception desk told me you wanted to speak with me." A man in a dark suit, white shirt, and royal blue tie stood in the doorway of his office. He took off his glasses and cleaned them with the handkerchief he drew out of his breast pocket.

"I'm Detective Donovan, and this is Miss O'Malley."

Daisy watched the woman back away from the elevator. She leaned toward the manager, trying to hear what he said.

The children began to fight. "Be quiet, children. I'm trying to listen."

"Sibyl, move. The elevator is here," her husband said.

Daisy watched the elevator bounce, and the door slid open.

"Oh, all right. Come on." The woman dragged the children into the elevator.

Jack turned back to the manager when the elevator closed. "Have you heard Charles Miller has been murdered on the beach in one of the rented boats in front of this hotel? Was he coming to do business with you?"

"I don't want to admit this, but he was one of our suppliers of bootleg alcohol. However, I didn't expect him tonight."

"Do you know anything about why someone would want to murder him, or about his business, or connections to the Mafia?"

"What do you mean?"

"Did you know that besides alcohol, drugs come off the boats in the Pacific?"

The manager began to wipe the sweat forming on his forehead with his handkerchief. "I have no idea about drugs. Today I didn't even have a shipment of alcohol coming in from him… And I certainly don't deal in the drug trade. I have no idea why he was here." He dabbed the beads of sweat beginning to form on his forehead again. "I don't know anything about him. I bring in very little alcohol from him. For most of our alcohol, I use a company from the east coast. It comes from the southern part of the state by truck." He pushed his handkerchief into his jacket pocket. "How was he killed?"

"A gunshot to the head." Jack watched the manager carefully. "His car was found near the tunnel to the kitchen. Did you hear a gunshot?"

"No, but there is a lot of commotion in the kitchen. Pots and pans clanging, chefs shouting. You can imagine the noise. It's anything but quiet."

"Do you mind if we talk to the kitchen staff?"

"No. They work in shifts, so there is always someone in the kitchen twenty-four hours a day. Please come with me." He pulled out his handkerchief again and wiped his forehead again as he led them to the back of the hallway, opened the door, and walked them down a flight of stairs to the kitchen. "The shift that's in the kitchen now would probably have been there when the victim was shot."

Jack and Daisy followed the manager. He pushed through a swinging door. They entered a large room with chefs and kitchen help busily preparing food. The staff peeled vegetables. They fried, roasted, and boiled food—several people in the corner of the room decorated desserts.

"Where does the heavy metal door go at the back of the room?" Jack pointed to the back wall. "Does it go to the tunnel?"

"Yes, Shipments come through there. It has to be heavy to keep out the small amount of water that pools outside it at high tide. It's so heavy, and with the noise inside, probably nothing could be heard through it."

Jack put his fingers to his lips and whistled a shrill whistle at the staff. When they quieted down, the manager shouted at them. "The detective wants to ask you some questions."

A man in whites and a toque (chef's hat) on his head yelled at two of the staff still talking to each other, quieting them. He knocked the spoon out of the hand of the man next to him. "Pay attention."

"You'll have to excuse the chef. He's a bit high strung," the hotel manager whispered.

"Did anyone hear a gunshot a little while ago or see Charles Miller?"

"Who is Charles Miller?" asked the Chef.

Everyone in the kitchen looked at each other and shook their heads.

"Did anyone see someone who didn't belong in here?"

They all shook their heads again.

"Okay, go back to work." He turned to the manager. "Let's go back upstairs."

"Have you ever seen Miller with anybody nefarious in the restaurant?"

"A group was here a couple of nights ago. Miller was with them."

"Did they fight with Miller?"

"They didn't make any trouble, but they seemed unhappy with him. I heard him say he would get them their money. He stormed out of the restaurant. A rather burly man followed him."

Jack turned to the manager. "Thanks. If you or your staff think of anything, call me." Jack handed him his card. "I'm at the police station in Hollywood."

"I will. Can you find your way back? I have to discuss a few things with the chef."

"Sure. Come on, Daisy." He led her to the staircase and out the front door of the hotel.

"Do you think the manager was telling the truth?" Daisy asked as they left the hotel basement and walked to the murder site.

"About what?"

"Everything."

"I doubt it, but he's protected by the District Attorney and police like every other person who has connections with criminals. The actors in Hollywood bring in a lot of money to the city. All the businesses profit from this money. The chef wasn't telling the truth about Miller. He checks all the food and drinks coming into the kitchen. The Mafia is not only in Hollywood and the film business, and restaurants, but in the hotels too."

She glanced at her watch. "Speaking of actors, I have to get back to the set. My scene is almost ready to be filmed. They're filming at night for this scene." She wanted to see if anyone knew about the murder. "Do you think one of the policemen, who is still here, could give me a ride?"

"I'll get someone to take you." He looked around.

"Hey, Steve, get over here."

"Yes, Chief."

"Please take Miss O'Malley to her set. Then get back here."

"See you tomorrow tonight at about eight. We'll go back to the speakeasy."

"I'll be ready."

"Thank you." Daisy leaned over and kissed his cheek. "Oops, sorry. I just get excited." She laughed. "Please take this." She handed him the small plastic package she had been carrying in her pocket. "I'm afraid I might lose it."

He smiled and hugged her.

She turned to the policeman. "It won't take long to get to where I need to go. It's at the corner of Mayberry and Stone. Down the street from Walsh's house." *It will probably always be known as the Walsh house even when another owner comes along.*

She held on to the seat as the policeman sped from the hotel. When they reached the address she'd given to the policeman, the street was empty, except for the equipment for filming the movie and a western stage set.

He turned to Daisy as he slid to a stop. "No one is here."

"Well, I guess I'm early. You can leave me."

"I'm not sure I should leave you here," the policeman said. "The chief will be upset if I leave you all alone."

"See, there's Mary Giroux. I'm not alone." She pointed to the woman standing in the shadows and talking on the phone sitting on a table.

"I'm not sure."

"Don't worry. Everyone will be here soon. I'll be fine. It will give me a chance to study my lines." *Again, a little white lie won't hurt. He doesn't have to know the truth. If he thinks I'm going to study, he'll leave me and won't report to Jack.*

"All right but be careful while you wait."

"I will." She jumped out of the patrol car and watched him pull away. "I wonder why she's here," Daisy whispered. Trying to get closer, she crept onto the set and hid behind the fake front of a barn. She listened.

"Mother, I'm coming to Venice Beach. I'm not going to let you hurt me anymore. I found out you went to see Desmond. I know that's why he wouldn't marry me. You interfered." Mary slammed down the receiver and ran to the corner of the set. She stood waving. A limo pulled from the shadows. The driver jumped out and opened the back door.

Daisy heard her say. "Venice Beach."

"I need to change my clothes." Daisy waited until the patrol car was at the end of the street and turned the corner. She crossed the street, walked to the main street, and waited. Finally, she saw a taxicab driving toward her. She waved for it to stop. Jumping in the backseat, she leaned forward. "The hotel at the end of the street."

"Lady, that's one block."

"I need you to stop there and wait while I change."

When the cab stopped, she leaped out. "I'll only be about five minutes. Keep the meter running." She threw the words over her shoulder as she ran towards the front door of the hotel. She reached the front desk and retrieved her key. Not waiting for the elevator, she ran up the stairs. Out of breath, she stood, for a moment, breathing heavily. Unlocking and opening the door to her room, she glanced around. No ghosts. Still out of breath, she leaned on the door and rested for another moment. "Okay, I have to get going."

She tossed Jack's jacket on the bed and pulled off her dress. She dumped it on the bed and quickly changed into casual clothes. She looked at Jack's jacket. "I forgot to give it back. Well, he won't need it until tomorrow." Looking in the mirror, she laughed. Her headband with the feathers was still on her head. *Doesn't quite go with slacks and a sweater.* She stuck it in the drawer and quickly ran a brush through her hair. "That's better." She ran down the stairs. She looked out the revolving door at the curb in front of the hotel. *Thank goodness, the cab is still here. I knew I could count on him.*

Jumping into the backseat of the cab, she leaned forward. "Venice Beach. The beginning of the main canal, please." She leaned back and inhaled and exhaled. "And hurry."

The driver sped through the streets. When he reached the boardwalk, she handed him his fee, plus a great deal extra, and jumped out of the taxi.

"Thanks, Lady," he yelled.

She crossed the boardwalk and ran down the steps to the boat dock. She stared at a man in long, tan pants held up by dark suspenders and a white, stained undershirt. His left foot stood on a bench next to a group of boats. In his right hand, he held a pipe. Puffing on it, he blew the smoke into air.

"Are you still working?" she asked. Daisy looked at the water's edge and watched the sand swirl as the tide moved out.

"I remember you. You were with the police the other day."

"Yes. That was me."

"Miss, where do you want to go?"

"To the blue house on the Grand Canal near the lagoon."

"I just brought someone out there."

"Was it a woman?"

"Yup, and she was pretty upset."

"Take me to the house, please."

"I'll get you there. Hop in. You'll be my last trip of the evening." The Boatman loosened the boat's line from the group of ropes that tied the boats to a pole in the sand. He dragged the boat to the edge of the water.

She jumped into the boat as he pushed it into the water.

He looked at her over his shoulder as he rowed. "You must be back in forty-five minutes. My shift is over. If you aren't, you'll be stuck on the island until daybreak when the boats start to ferry people again," he yelled over the slapping of the waves on the side of the boat.

"It looks as if there's going to be a storm." She sat back and looked. "The is sky is getting dark. Clouds are beginning to move over the moon and stars."

"I'll be back on the dock in forty-five minutes. We have to be very quiet when we reach the dock. I don't want anyone to know I'm coming. It's a surprise." She looked at the waves as they hit the rocks and pilings of the dock.

"All right, Miss. Remember, forty-five minutes." He grabbed the dock and tied the boat to the end-post of the pier. "I'll only wait forty-five minutes."

CHAPTER THIRTEEN

Daisy pulled up her sleeve and glanced at her watch. "I will be back. I promise." She waved and crept from the dock and over the lawn to the front of the cottage. Bright house lights showed the silhouettes of three women, two standing and one in a wheelchair, against the drapes in front of the picture window in the main room. Their hands flailed, and their voices were loud and angry. She ducked into the bushes at the side of the bungalow. *It must be Charlotte and Mary and Beth.* Able to hear what they said, she listened.

The breeze lifted her hair. It flew around her face and shoulders. She tried to push it behind her ears, but several strands caught on a bush branch next to her. She stood very still and pulled on her hair, trying to untangle it. The motion made the branch bend, then crack. She bent down. It was the only thing she could do.

The screaming stopped.

"Be quiet. What was that? Did you hear something?" One of the voices close to the window shrieked. The drape was pulled away from the window. A face pressed against the glass.

"It's nothing, Mother. Probably an animal. Listen to me," Mary cried.

"Someone is out there. I'm sure of it."

"Forget it," Beth yelled. "I want you to listen to me."

The angry screaming started up again.

The drape dropped. Catching on something, it didn't close all the way. Daisy peeked in. She saw three women, Mary Giroux, her sister Beth, and their mother.

"Mother, they think I killed Desmond because he rejected me. I never got to say goodbye to him. I was so in love with him. We were going to marry. We were planning a future together."

"Shut up, Mary. Mother doesn't care," Beth shouted.

"Beth be quiet. Mary, you don't know what you're talking about. He was thirty years older than you. And do you know how many other women thought he was going to marry them? At least two more."

"I know you have a gun," Beth screamed. "If I tell the police, they'll look for it and do a real search. Then you'll be in trouble."

"I can tell them how you interfered with his love for me," Mary yelled.

"They can never prove anything. I got rid of my gun a long time ago," Charlotte screamed.

"You are not telling the truth. I saw it in my bedroom the other day," Beth shouted.

Daisy looked at her watch. She held it to the light coming from the window. *Oh no. I've been here an hour. The boatman is gone.* She slid down under a large bush. *Thank goodness, it's not too cold. I'll catch the first boat tomorrow.* She listened and watched more of the argument between Charlotte and her daughters.

"I've been your meal ticket and that of my sisters since I was five. I'm going to sue you for all the money you stole from me," Mary said.

"Don't be silly. You're too young to handle the money. I used it to pay all your expenses."

"Well, you have many antiques and lots of jewelry. You didn't work to get them."

Charlotte reached for her daughter and started to shake her.

Daisy realized they moved to the far end of the room. She stood and leaned against the windowpane and peered through the part not covered by the curtain.

"Stay away from me. Did you know Desmond and I were secretly engaged, and I'm carrying his child?"

"You can't be pregnant. You aren't telling the truth. If you are, I can take care of that. Don't you realize, or are you so blind you can't see, that he didn't act like an engaged man? I know you believed you were the only woman romantically involved with him, and he was in love with you. I'm telling you, dear, there was no outward evidence he returned your affection. He had other women. I never saw you in public with him. He would not have kept it a secret if he intended to marry you."

"Mother, you're domineering and manipulative. Just leave me alone. I'm going to bed."

"Mary, stop. The murder of Desmond Walsh appears every day in the newspapers. None of the articles name you as a suspect, or me."

"I mean it. You probably killed my only love, my friend. You're so crazy I bet you killed Charles Miller too." Mary's eyes streamed with tears.

"I'll back you," Beth screamed. "We'll fight her together. Mother will finally be punished."

"I'm going to report you to the police. I know you have a gun," Mary cried.

"Mary. Now you're acting crazy. Your sister lies about me because I favor you. Don't listen to a word she says."

Daisy stared. She watched Mary storm from the room. Her face was red with rage. Daisy watched for a minute. *Well, that's the end of that. I'll look for proof in the morning. I guess I'll try to sleep. I'll look for the gun tomorrow. The morning will be here soon.* She looked into the darkness and trembled with chills and fatigue. Sliding down into a space between the bushes, she curled up and closed her eyes.

Her relief was short-lived. She felt herself being grabbed from behind. An arm wound around her neck. She awoke instantly. The bushes scratched at her face. She was pulled to her feet. Stars burst in front of her eyes.

"What are you doing here?"

"The boatman dropped me on the wrong island. I was going to knock and see if I could get help. But I got tangled in the bushes." Daisy glimpsed over her shoulder.

Six feet of mostly muscle stood behind her. Charlotte's bodyguard wasn't fooled.

"We'll see about that. Move." He pushed her.

She turned, blindly stumbling, as he shoved her toward the front door. He pushed her up the front stairs of the cottage and banged his fist on the door.

The shouting stopped.

"Who is it?" Charlotte hollered.

"Open up," Hans yelled.

"Hans, it's late. Go to your cottage." Charlotte stared. She looked surprised when she threw open the door."

"I found this person on my rounds. She was hiding in the bushes." He shoved Daisy toward the front doorway.

The weather changed. The moon, having raised above the trees, was covered by clouds. The stars had disappeared. The sky was pitch black. The wind began to howl. A freak storm covered the island. Daisy nervously moistened her dry lips. The only thing she could see through the driving rain was the lights of Hollywood on the horizon. The wind thrashed around the palm trees and bushes. The trees palms bent, touching the ground. Thunder cracked and lightning whipped around the sky.

Daisy shivered, getting soaking wet.

"Get into the house." Hans gave her a push through the doorway. She hit the room wall. Charlotte stared at Daisy, dripping water on the dark, blue rug, with dark, angry eyes.

Mary ran from the bedroom into the room. "I found her gun, hidden in her closet. I'm giving it to you to give to the police."

"Mother, you're caught." Beth sat in her wheelchair, smiling.

"I'm sure she killed Desmond." Mary lifted her arm with the gun and turned toward Daisy.

Charlotte paled. "Mary, you're very mad at me. Don't tell lies. Don't be like your sister."

"I'm not lying."

Charlotte grabbed the gun from her daughter before she could give it to Daisy. She ran to the front door, threw it open, and tossed the gun into the bushes in front of the house.

Daisy heard a thud and a splash.

"Hans, we have to get rid of her." Charlotte looked down. She slammed the door shut.

"It landed in the mud around the bushes. I'll get it tomorrow after we take care of you." She spat out the words with contempt and glared at Daisy.

"Hans, hold your gun on her." Charlotte ran into the kitchen. She came back to the front room with a knife and rope. "Now tie her hands." Charlotte held the knife close to Daisy's neck.

Daisy felt the rope bite into her wrists. She heard crying and turned her head. Mary cowered in the corner of the room. Tears streamed down her cheeks.

Beth sat silently next to her sister. Suddenly she screamed. "Don't worry Daisy, we'll take care of our mother." Her mouth formed a sneer.

"Charlotte. Did you kill Desmond Walsh?" Daisy kept her eyes on the woman's hands.

The color drained from Charlotte's face. Her eyes were hooded like a hawk. "All right. I'll tell you. It doesn't matter now. You won't be around to tell anyone." Anger lit up her eyes. "Mary didn't know that I knew about the letters. Charles Miller told me about them." Her lips twisted into a cynical smile. "I talked to Desmond on the phone and begged him to give me the letters Mary wrote to him. He wouldn't listen to me. Someone came into the house while I was talking to him, and he hung up."

That must have been when Mabel Vidor came to the house. Daisy stared at the woman.

"I was so mad. I had Hans drive me to Desmond's house. Desmond was with Mabel Vidor when I arrived. I wore slacks, a long coat, scarf, and hat so no one would recognize me. I waited on the patio until Mabel's car left, and the valet left. I brought the gun to scare him. I burst into the house and asked him if he was going to marry you. He laughed and said he would never marry you. Mary, did you hear me? He was never going to marry you."

Mary began to sob.

"I got so angry that I shook the gun in his face. He stood between the couch and the coffee table and held up his hands. He turned his back to me. He had the nerve to say, 'Go ahead and shoot. I dare you.' I lost it and shot. I didn't mean to shoot him. I ran from the house right away."

Daisy took a deep breath.

"Somehow, Charles Miller found out. I don't know how. He was always around Desmond. Maybe he was in the house and hid when I came. He tried to blackmail me. After one payment, I knew it would never stop…

"Hans helped me kill him. We lured him to the boats that row people around the islands. We told him to be there at 12:30 a.m. because the tide would be coming in, and there would be no boatmen there. He parked his car on the dirt road next to the tunnel and near my house. Hans and I met him on the road and walked, through the sand, with him to the boats." She sneered. "We told him we would take a boat and go into the lagoon where no one would see us. Hans sat next to him. I sat behind them," she shouted.

"We pretended we were going to pay him and were making plans for a place to leave the money after I got it. While Hans spoke to him about the plans, I took out my gun and shot him." She stared at Daisy.

"Why are you telling her?" Hans yelled.

"It doesn't matter. She won't be able to tell anyone. She'll be dead." Charlotte gave Daisy a push. "Start walking. Get to the door." She kept talking. "We only had one problem. We were going to push the boat out to sea, but we heard someone coming and had to leave. We decided to hide under the boardwalk until he left, but he called the police. There was so much commotion we escaped with no one seeing us." Her lips spread into a thin smile. "Imagine, Charles thought he could get money from me." She laughed.

"Mother, what are you going to do?" Mary said through uncontrollable sobs.

"She's going to commit another murder," Beth yelled.

Tears slowly found their way down Mary's cheek.

"Don't worry. We'll take care of Miss Daisy, and you girls can go on with your lives. Go to your room." Charlotte opened the front door and gave Daisy a shove. "Move."

The rain had slowed to a drizzle, but the front porch was wet. Daisy slipped on the top step. She lost her balance and fell. A pain shot through her as her hip caught the side of the step. She bounced to the bottom of the staircase.

"Get up and walk." Charlotte's voice was cold and exact.

Daisy tasted blood and felt the split in her lip with her shaking fingers. Her feet and clothes were wet. The mud seeped into her shoes on the dirt road and filled with sand and water when she reached the beach. A shiver spread over her. *The tide is coming in.*

"Here we are. Get next to the jetty."

Daisy leaned on the rocks of the jetty. She looked around at the stone wall. *It's useless, no one will hear me. The waves hitting the beach and large boulders as the tide comes in will prevent anyone from hearing my voice, even if I yell.*

"Sit down," Hans shouted, shoving Daisy.

Daisy was tempted to run, but Charlotte still held a knife.

Charlotte's mouth pulled into a sour grin. Her temper soared. Her eyes blazed. "Hans, tie her feet and cover her eyes with this blindfold." She pulled a huge handkerchief from her pocket.

Daisy heard the sound of the wind and the moving water coming through the opening in the jetty. As the water washed toward her she began to shake. The fear of drowning built in her mind.

"The tide is coming in. Try to sleep. It will be easier on you when the water covers you." Charlotte laughed.

Daisy didn't see Hans and Charlotte turn and walk to the boardwalk, but she knew they were leaving her.

Daisy heard Charlotte's voice in the distance. "It won't be long. We'll be home free."

Daisy's breath cut off.

Charlotte laughed again. She walked up the stairs to the boardwalk. "Goodbye, my dear." Her voice hardened.

Daisy sucked in a breath and let it out with a shudder. Fear knotted in her stomach and swept through her. She couldn't control her spasmodic trembling. She clenched her teeth and tried to relax. She rubbed the knot of her blindfold against the stone wall. It fell off.

"Please don't leave me, please," she screamed. A cold shiver spread over her.

Charlotte was too far away for Daisy to hear Charlotte's conversation with Hans. "Come on, Hans, let's go have a drink and celebrate." She chuckled nastily.

Daisy's heart jumped in her chest. She took deep breaths and tried to think. *What should I do?* She felt the spray of water splashing on her thighs. *I have to get my brain in gear.*

A sixth sense brought her fully awake. Startled, she heard someone in the distance, calling her name. She listened to a voice yelling, "Daisy, Daisy."

"I'm here, I'm here," she yelled back. Someone yelled her name again. Panic welled in her throat when the voice stopped. She laid back against the jetty wall while tears ran down her cheeks. She waited. In a minute, she thrust herself against the rocks and pushed with her feet and legs. The stone wall dug into her skin. Standing, she jumped through the rising water in the lagoon. She struggled. Her feet splashed and sank into the sand with each jump. Then, she heard banging on a door and a voice coming from the direction of the Miles house.

Someone yelled. "Charlotte Miles, let us in."

"That's Jack." Daisy recognized his voice. "He's here, thank goodness." She waited and listened.

"Let us in."

Mary, let them in and tell Jack where I am. Daisy tried to transmit her thoughts to the girl. She didn't realize it worked.

Mary came to the door. "Please help us."

"Where is Daisy?" Jack yelled.

"I don't know. The bodyguard and my mother walked down the beach with her. My mother is crazy. She committed the murders. Her bodyguard helped her. And the gun is in the bushes next to the front porch."

"Call the paramedics."

"Don't leave us alone," Mary cried.

"I'm here. I'll help you." Beth smiled. "We have to stick together. It's you and me against Mother."

"I'm leaving a man here to look after you. He'll keep out of sight. If your mother comes back, don't tell her the police are here."

He yelled to his men. "Come with me." He turned and ran along the beach next to the house calling Daisy's name.

Daisy began to yell when she heard her name called. "I'm at the jetty." A cry of relief broke from her lips as the voice calling her name got closer. When she stared at the rocks, she saw a tall, dark figure step from the shadows. Jack's profile showed against the moonlight, now shining. The clouds had moved, and the rain stopped. He ran toward her through splashing water.

"Are you all right?" He rushed to her.

"I'm fine, just a little wet. My back probably has some scratches." She felt stiff and cold. She ran her hand through her hair. "My hair is a mess."

"Please. You almost drowned, and you're worried about your hair. I don't believe it."

He pulled off the ropes around her arms and legs, wrapped his jacket around her, and picked her up.

"How did you know I was here?" Warmth crept slowly into her body.

"The boatman who brought you over to the island got worried when you didn't come back to the dock and the boat on time. He was sure you would because you promised to be back in forty-five minutes. When you didn't show up, he immediately called the police." He stared at her. "Why did you come here?"

"When I left you and went to the movie set, I saw Mary Giroux. She was talking on the phone. After she hung up, I heard her call her driver and ordered him to take her to the boardwalk. She was in tears. I decided to follow her to see if I could find out why she was so upset," she told him as he carried her back to the house. "Did you see Charlotte and her bodyguard?"

"No. I left a man at the house to watch for them."

Daisy saw the policeman walk out of the bushes.

"They're in the house, Chief." The police joined them at the staircase of the front porch.

Jack put Daisy next to the policeman, climbed the stairs, stood at the front door, and knocked. "Mrs. Miles?"

"Yes, detective?" she asked as she opened the door. "This is a busy place tonight. Miss O'Malley was here, but she left a long time ago."

Charlotte turned to her bodyguard. "Put the gun down, Hans. Hans just has the gun to protect me."

Two policemen entered the house, pushed past her, and grabbed the bodyguard.

"Okay, boys, put the handcuffs on them." Jack looked at Charlotte Miles and her bodyguard. "Miss O'Malley is standing at the bottom of your porch. We know what you tried to do. You're both under arrest for the murders of Desmond Walsh and Charles Miller and the attempted murder of Daisy O'Malley."

He looked at Mary. "Can you get me a blanket?"

Mary ran to the bedroom and returned with an afghan.

"Take these people to the station. The boatman is waiting. I'll be right there," he said to one of the policemen while he wrapped Daisy in the blanket. "We'll take your statements tomorrow morning. Mary, come to the station about nine."

"Me too," Beth cried. "Now, I can get back at Mother for treating me so badly."

"I'll be there. Don't worry." Mary's voice was firm. "We'll find the gun and bring it with us. The paramedics said they would be waiting at the boardwalk."

Jack looked at Daisy. "I won't yell at you now, because everything worked out. Next time, call me. Do you know what could have happened to you?" He shook his head.

"Yes." She didn't add, *and no one in my time would ever figure out what happened to me. She would just be a missing person for eternity.* "I'm sorry. I'll stick to acting." She shivered with chill and fatigue.

CHAPTER FOURTEEN

Hollywood, 1922

Thank you for helping me escape death," Daisy said as they rode back to the boardwalk in the boat. "I have something to tell you. Maybe we can sit on the dock."

"Let's get back to the hotel so you can get changed into dry clothes. Then you can tell me anything you want to."

She went through different scenarios in her head about coming from 2018 on the drive to the hotel. None of them seemed right. She twisted her earring.

Reaching the hotel, he followed her into the lobby. "I'll wait here." He sat in one of the chairs.

"I won't be long." She picked up her key and ran to the elevator. It had just landed on the first floor. She waited for the passengers to exit and entered. No ghosts were around. "Three, please."

She quickly showered and dressed in her jeans, sweater, and boots. After stuffing the 1920's clothes into shopping bags, she looked at them. "I'll never wear all these clothes. I'll donate them," she whispered.

She was ready to tell Jack who she really was. It was time. The case was over. Daisy smiled at the elevator operator and ran her tale over in her mind once more.

When she reached the lobby, Jack was reading the paper. "Any change in the news about the murder?" she asked.

"Not yet. The reporters hanging around the police station are probably just getting the news." He smiled. "So, what is it you have to tell me?" Jack dragged his fingers through his hair.

"I don't quite know how to explain what I'm about to tell you. I've run what I have to say a million different ways in my mind." She let out a long sigh. "I even practiced some of them in front of the mirror. I've finally decided the only way to tell you is to blurt it out." Her brows drew together.

Jack stared at her. "Keep going." His mouth curved into an unconscious smile.

She looked straight into his eyes. "You won't have to worry about me anymore." Her voice drifted into a hushed whisper. "I'm from another time, the year 2018. I don't know how I got here. It has something to do with the gazebo. It's magical. When I get in it, a mist covers the area. I can go back and forth between 1922 and my time, 2018." She sighed. "I'm not sure why I've come into your time. I know you don't want to come into my world. I don't want to say goodbye, but I don't want to leave my family and daughter. I would have to do that if I stayed here." She smiled. "I believe we will meet again in another lifetime."

A light passed between them. He was momentarily speechless. His gaze became as soft as a caress. When he spoke, his voice was tender. "Somehow, I always thought there was something very special about you..." He stared at her. "Possibly, all we are is all we're meant to be, very good friends. Though, I'm losing a good partner. We could conquer and clean up the crime here in 1922. However, it wasn't meant to be." He looked into her eyes. "You're right. I know we'll meet in another time."

She saw the heart-rending tenderness of his gaze. It wrapped her in an invisible warmth. Her heart ached. A sadness that their day was ending gripped her heart.

"We can remember a wonderful friendship." He smiled. Turning, he whispered. "I hate goodbyes." He walked slowly from the hotel.

She waited until he went through the front door of the hotel, then rode in the elevator to her room.

Daisy was dressed in the clothes she wore the day she came to Hollywood and slipped into 1922. Her boots felt good. She really didn't like the 1922 shoes. *I think I'll keep some of the 20's clothes.* She pulled a few from the bag and folded them. She packed them in the bag she bought from the boutique. She repacked the others and put them back in the shopping bags. Taking a last look around her room, she gathered up the suitcase and shopping bags, and closed the door.

Standing in front of the elevator, she waited. A voice called to her. She looked in its direction and saw the ghost of Desmond Walsh standing at the end of the hall. She watched him smile and wave. Daisy heard him whisper, "Thank you."

A tear formed in her eye and she wiped it away with the back of her hand and waved. Taking her last ride down the elevator from the third floor, she walked to the reception desk, paid her bill, and returned her key. She smiled. "My visit to your hotel was wonderful. Would you mind delivering these clothes and makeup to the church down the street?" She handed him the shopping bags.

"No, Miss. I'd be glad to. Please pay us another visit soon." He waved as she slung her purse over her shoulder and strolled, with the brown leather carryon suitcase, to the revolving door.

She was surprised when she saw Jack. He was leaning against the door of his patrol car outside the hotel.

"We said our goodbyes last night." She smiled.

"I know," he answered. "I had to see you one more time."

It was hard for her to say goodbye. She would miss Jack, but they were from different times.

"Let me walk you to the gazebo." He wrapped his arm around her waist as they walked.

When they reached the gazebo, Daisy put down her luggage and hugged him. She saw him look at her as if he were photographing her with his eyes. "It's time." A tear ran down her cheek. She gathered her purse and luggage and ran up the stairs of the gazebo. She sat on the bench. Within minutes a mist rolled over the lawn and gazebo, engulfing the bench. "Goodbye," her voice echoed through the mist.

California, 2018

When the mist cleared, Daisy saw the apothecary and a picture of herself on a poster tacked to a street pole. Luckily, a taxi sat on the street in front of the pole. She waved to the driver and crossed the street. Digging into her purse, she pulled out her sunglasses and pushed them up on the bridge of her nose.

He started his motor and inched his cab to her. Leaning over, he rolled down the window on the passenger side and yelled over his radio that blasted a 1960 song. "Where to, Lady?"

"To the police station down the street and then LAX, please."

The driver threw open his door and jumped from his seat. He ran to the curb, opened the back door, and grabbed her case. He slid it on the seat next to her after she got settled.

"The station is not too far away."

When he stopped, she opened her door. "I'll only be a minute." She hurried out of the cab. Running up a flight of stairs, she stopped at the front desk. "Sergeant."

"Yes, Miss." A computer sat on the desk. She glanced around the room. It looked much different than the 1922 station. There was new equipment, but the desk of the Sergeant was battered.

"I've seen the posters. I'm the woman you are looking for. I forgot to tell my driver I was going to the mountains for a week. He must have been upset when I disappeared."

He stared at her. "Lady, the poor man was beside himself. You actresses are all alike. You have to be more careful and tell people where you are going and when."

"Yes, sir. You don't know how bad I feel. Can I write him a note in case he comes by here to see if I've been found? Never mind, I'll call him on my phone." She pulled open her purse and hunted for her cell phone. Finding it, she glanced at the amount of time she had left to talk. *Thank goodness, I have enough power to send him a message.*

She began to punch in his number as she ran to the back door of the taxi. *It went to voice mail. I'll leave a message.* "John. This is Daisy O'Malley. Sorry I didn't tell you about my trip. Going back to Maine, so won't need you anymore. Will send you a final check. Please contact a real-estate agent and send me her name. I want to put my house on the market. Thank you for all your good work. You've been a big help to me while in Hollywood. I will miss you." *I'm sorry I can't tell him what happened to me.* "Please pack up my things and send them to my address in Maine."

"Okay, I'm ready to go to the airport." She jumped into the taxi.

The driver turned down his radio as he drove. "Leaving Hollywood for good or a vacation?"

"I'm leaving for good." Daisy looked down at her case. "I'm going back home. I miss my daughter and family."

He peered at her intently in the rearview mirror. "You're traveling light."

"I had my clothes shipped."

"A lot of people come here and leave soon after they arrive. Lots of them turn to drugs and alcohol. You seem okay."

Things haven't changed since the Twenties. There are still drugs, alcohol, and crazy lifestyles. "I have a family waiting for me." She smiled.

"Where does your family live?"

"Well, three of my sisters live in Europe, but my twin lives in Maine. That's where I'm going."

"When's your flight?"

"I don't have a ticket yet, but there's a plane leaving in three hours." She glanced at her watch. "I guess it's…two and a half now. I hope I'll be able to get a seat. I'm excited about going home."

"Which airline?"

"Just drop me at the Delta departure door."

The cab slid to the curb outside the entrance; she dug into her pocket, pulled out a tip and fare, and handed him the money. "Thanks."

"Thank you. Have a safe trip."

At the reservation counter, Daisy stood in a long line behind the white line. Finally, it was her turn. She rushed to the counter. "Are there any seats left on the flight to Boston and then on a flight to Maine?"

"Yes, you've gotten the last seat to Boston. It's in business class. Is that okay?"

"That's fine. It's a long flight. Might as well be comfortable."

"The flight to Maine is filled, but you can stay overnight in a hotel at Boston's Logan Airport and get the first plane to Maine tomorrow. It will be one of those small twenty-seater planes."

"Okay." Daisy slid her credit card and license across the counter. As the clerk, processed up the tickets.

"Luggage?"

"No, just a carry on?"

"The transport will take you. The plane is starting to board."

Daisy hopped on the cart. "Flight 349. Terminal C. I believe they are boarding." Daisy sat with her carryon in her lap. The driver beeped his horn at the people walking in front of him. He drove at top speed to the gate.

She reached the plane as the door was about to close. Tipping the driver, she ran to the agent, and handed him her ticket. After he scanned it, she continued to the jet-way, through the plane door, and down the aisle to her seat. Stuffing her case into the overhead, she slid past the passenger in the aisle seat and sat in the window seat. "Sorry."

"Oh, my goodness." She sat and stared at the man in the seat next to her. A gasp escaped her. It wasn't Jack, but he could have been Jack's twin.

"Is something wrong?" He looked up from his magazine and smiled.

"No. You look just like a friend of mine."

"They say everyone has a double."

The ping of the seatbelt sign came on. Daisy buckled up and leaned back as the plane taxied on the runway and lifted off. The plane soared through the clouds to Boston. Looking out of the window, she watched the large letters of the Hollywood sign fade. She threw it a kiss and whispered. "Thanks for the great adventure."

"What? Did you say something?"

"No. I'm Daisy O'Malley." She extended her hand.

"Lucas Donovan."

"I know I said this before, but you look so familiar." *He has Jack's dark hair and eyes and his strong, capable, and honest look.* She felt an immediate bond with him.

"You must have seen me around Hollywood or in the papers. I represent actors and actresses in difficult cases. My great-grandfather was a detective in Hollywood. That's why I got interested in law and helping to defend some of Hollywood's innocent people. And you?"

"What was your great-grandfather's name?"

"Jack Donovan. People say I look just like him. He's gone now, but I'll never forget him."

"Maybe that's where I've seen you, in the papers. I did some research on an old murder case in 1922. It was about the murder of a Hollywood director. If your grandfather was on the case, I must have seen his picture in the newspaper." *I don't know him. I can't tell him the real story.*

"And you? When you weren't doing research, what were you doing in Hollywood?"

"I was trying my luck at acting, but it was slow going. I got an offer to head the Drama Department at the University of Maine. I decided to take the job. Some of my family and my daughter are in Maine, and I miss them."

"I'm originally from California. Now I am the head of the law department at the University of Maine in Portland. I've fallen in love with the state and the East Coast. I'm not planning to live in California again. I plan to stay put in Maine. Besides, I can never get enough lobster."

Daisy smiled. "I can't get enough either, and I'm from there. My father had lobster pots, and we had lobster several times a week." She smiled. "What were you doing in California?"

"I'm a Dean but teach a few classes where all the students think they are Alan Dershowitz. Sometimes I get bored, and occasionally, I take a difficult case in California. I was involved in one between a Californian and a company in Washington, D.C. I'm glad it's finally over."

Daisy enjoyed herself as they talked. Before she knew it, the "fasten seat belt" sign flashed on. She held on to the armrest as the plane descended. When the landing wheels dropped, she closed her eyes. The plane rushed to a stop and then taxied slowly to the gate. She felt him touch her hand and opened her eyes.

"We're here," he said as he picked up his briefcase and stood. "Can I help you?" He reached for her case in the overhead bin.

"Thank you." She followed him to the bus and into the hotel.

"Since we have to stay the night at the Boston Airport Hilton, would you like to have dinner with me?" Lucas asked as they finished checking into the hotel.

"I would love to," she said, entering the elevator with him.

"What floor?"

"Three."

"Me too."

"Good. I'll meet you at eight in the dining room."

Slipping her card in the door lock, she waved. "See you later."

Daisy felt tired when she got to her room. *I can't wear sequins for dinner. Slacks, a blouse, and a sweater will do. I'll put on a fancy scarf.* She pulled out her 1920s clothes and laid them on the bed. *A power nap and a long shower will revive me.*

After her nap, she hopped into the shower. When the water cooled, she dried herself with one of the hotel's large fluffy towels, dressed, and applied her makeup carefully. She smiled when she met Lucas and laughed when he said, "Is it lobster for dinner?"

"Of course. I've been thinking about lobster since I got on the plane in LA."

They picked up their conversation from the plane and didn't stop talking until they said good night.

"I'll see you on the airport bus." He pulled her to him and hugged her.

"Sleep well." She smiled. *I can't believe how much he looks like Jack.* She slipped her key card into the lock. She couldn't deny the sparks of excitement she felt when she was with him. *I must have been with his great-grandfather when I helped with the investigation of the murder of Desmond Cunningham Walsh.*

On the flight the next day, she slid her carry-on under the seat in front of her. They both sat in aisle seats across from each other.

Again, their conversation picked up where they left off at dinner. When the plane landed in Portland, Lucas grabbed his case.

"My stop. Write your number on the back of my ticket cover. I'll let you get settled and call you." He handed her the ticket envelope and pulled a pen from his breast pocket.

"I'll be looking forward to your call." She wrote her phone number quickly. Handing the envelope and pen back to him, she waved. She couldn't deny there was a definite spark of excitement at the prospect of seeing him again.

Bar Harbor, Maine

Daisy looked out of the window. Her face lit up when she saw her mother, sister, Violet, and her daughter, Emily waiting for her at the gate of the small but noisy airport. She was happy to be home. She didn't plan to leave her childhood home again. She waited for the plane to stop, picked up her carry-on, and walked down the airplane steps to the tarmac. She was thrilled. The hugs and smiles didn't stop for a good ten minutes.

Her sister, who now lived with Emily and her husband in the gray Victorian, begged her to stay with them. Daisy moved into her old bedroom in the family home.

The gray Victorian never seemed to be so beautiful, Daisy thought.

Six Months Later

Lucas hadn't waited very long to call. After their first real date, the air around her seemed electrified. She saw him every weekend. Every time she saw him, the pull grew stronger. Sometimes Emily was with them. Her daughter and Lucas got along and liked each other. Daisy was in love and fell more and more in love with him each time they were together.

One Saturday afternoon, Lucas took her on a picnic to the beach in front of the Victorian home. They sat in front of the rocky bluff on a blanket covering the sand. At dessert, he withdrew a small, light blue box from the basket.

Her heart began to hammer in her ears when she watched him lift the lid. She saw a beautiful emerald surrounded by small diamonds.

"It belonged to my mother." He smiled. "Will you marry me?"

A soft gasp escaped her. Her heart sang with delight. The warmth of her smile echoed in her voice. "Yes." She smiled. "It is beautiful. Yes, I'll marry you. I'll never take it off." She stood.

"I want everyone in your family who's in the area to come to Portland for a celebration dinner next weekend."

"That will be wonderful. We'll all come." She couldn't keep her eyes off her ring.

The week went by quickly. When Daisy walked into the restaurant and to the table Lucas reserved, she was surprised. A man stood behind Lucas. She stared. He looked the same, but his brown hair had turned white. Age lines creased in his eyes and mouth. He winked at her. She knew no one else saw Lucas's great-grandfather, except her. She smiled when he faded into the wall behind the table.

After they ordered their dinners, Lucas began to talk. "I found a photo in some papers belonging to my great-grandfather. It was a picture of my grandfather and a young woman who looks very much like Daisy.

He used to tell me stories about his life, as a detective in California, when I was a young boy. One of the stories he told me was about meeting a woman he would never forget. When I saw the picture, I knew Daisy, and I were meant to be."

The ghost of Jack Donavan appeared behind his grandson, again. He lifted his hand and waved. He winked at Daisy as he approached her. Leaning close to her, he whispered. "You can tell him someday of your ability to go back in time and meeting me. Don't tell him right now."

After dinner, when the family members attending the dinner left, she walked with Lucas to his apartment. She sat in front of the fire burning on the hearth.

"My family has a clam bake at this time every year. I hope you won't be traveling and will be there. You'll get to meet everyone in my family. My sisters and their families will come from Europe."

"Of course. I wouldn't miss it. If I had a trip, I would cancel it."

A few days later, Daisy and Lucas stood on the top step of the Victorian. Home. All of Daisy's sisters, their husbands, and children were there. The main topic of the clam bake was her wedding. She stretched out her left hand and watched her engagement ring sparkle in the bright sun. She was happy. Her life was wonderful. The past was over and forgotten.

The End

A Taste of
THE ROARING TWENTIES

Grilled Sweet Potato Slices

1 pound sweet potatoes cut into ¼ inch thick slices
Cooking spray
1 Tablespoon barbecue seasoning
¼ cup crumbled blue cheese

Coat potatoes with spray and sprinkle with seasoning.
Grill over indirect heat 4-5 minutes on each side or until
tender. Place on serving dish and sprinkle with blue
cheese.

Shrimp and Raviolis

1 package of spinach and cheese raviolis
1 1/2 pounds raw jumbo shrimp, shells and tails removed
1 medium yellow squash
1 medium zucchini squash
1 medium onion
1 lemon and dill prepared sauce from grocery store.
Oil as needed

Thin slice vegetables and fry for five minutes. Don't
brown Add lemon dill sauce, then add raviolis to pan.
Cook five minutes. Add shrimp and cook until shrimp are
done.
Serve with a salad.

Did you enjoy *Daisy, In Our Mother's Garden, Book Five*? If so, please help us spread the word about Joyce Humphrey Cares.

• Recommend the book to your family and friends

• Post a review on retail sites and Goodreads

• Tweet and Facebook about it

ABOUT THE AUTHOR

Joyce Humphrey Cares lives in Central Florida. A voracious reader since childhood, she finally decided to take a stab at writing. She combines her love of history and the places she has traveled when she weaves her stories.

When she is not writing, Joyce is a Guardian ad litem volunteer, builds and decorates dollhouses, plays golf, and plans her next trip to a place where she can return home and write a romantic suspense or time travel story.

She is a member of Romance Writers of America, and the Florida chapter of Mystery Writers of America.

She may be contacted at joycecares01@gmail.com or at her webpage www.joycehumphreycares.com.

Other Books
It Started With Forbidden Love
It Happened Yesterday
Beyond the Mist
Degrees of Wickedness
Violet, In Our Mother's Garden, Book One
Lily, In Our Mother's Garden, Book Two
Rose, In Our Mother's Garden, Book Three
Iris, In Our Mother's Garden, Book Four